DOME OF THE ROCK

Chad Taylor

PublishAmerica
Baltimore

© 2008 by Chad Taylor.
All rights reserved. No part of this book may be reproduced, stored in a retrieval system or transmitted in any form or by any means without the prior written permission of the publishers, except by a reviewer who may quote brief passages in a review to be printed in a newspaper, magazine or journal.

First printing

All characters in this book are fictitious, and any resemblance to real persons, living or dead, is coincidental.

PublishAmerica has allowed this work to remain exactly as the author intended, verbatim, without editorial input.

ISBN: 1-60672-509-2
PUBLISHED BY PUBLISHAMERICA, LLLP
www.publishamerica.com
Baltimore

Printed in the United States of America

CHAPTER 1

In every person's life there is a defining moment, something that makes them the person they were destined to become. Each of us faces an obstacle we think impossible to overcome and beat back the demon that threatens to consume us. Whether it is as simple as asking out the pretty girl at the coffee shop or as difficult as learning to walk again after a car accident, we all have something we must face, something under the surface that we fear could overtake us and send us into a spiral that we may never recover from.

My father's demon turned out to be a little different. Dr. Seamus McCracken, Dad, wanted more than anything to uncover something that most people find laughable. The mere idea of what Dad wanted existing is beyond most people's accepted comprehension. What my father searched for in life was a simple answer to an impossible equation, a tangible site proving the existence of the afterlife here on Earth.

As I tell you this story, keep in mind that everything I tell you happened just as I have explained it. I'm not the type of person who embellishes my stories to impress others. I firmly believe in speaking the truth at all times, being completely forthright in my words and my actions. I learned from the best, my father, how to carry oneself, and to this day I still lead the life my father instilled in me.

CHAPTER 2

The first I heard of Dad's intentions came at our breakfast table when I was a senior in high school. We lived in a beautiful cottage, a nice Victorian manor under the shade of maples and pines in the small town of Brandh, Maine. Brandh was a quiet village nestled about halfway between Bangor and Bar Harbor, just miles from the Atlantic and meters from Brandh Lake, a sparkling blue pool that served as both a cool refuge from the heat of summer and a great hockey rink in winter. Everyone that lived in Brandh, all three hundred or so of us, enjoyed the Maple Days in May and the Blueberry Fair in September. Life in that little cottage within that quaint town's limits was sweet.

Every day, Dad would drop me at Brandh High School and I would sit in classes, learning about economics or English or math. Friday nights in the fall meant Black Bears football; we finished with six wins and three losses my senior year. Almost every male played football at Brandh, all forty-three of us. We even had a female kicker my senior year, Lacey Keyes. Winter meant basketball when hockey didn't take precedence. The spring was baseball time. I hurt my shoulder in football and decided to sit out these sports my senior year. Besides, my running skills were described as like a moose wearing galoshes by my closest friends.

Anyway, back to my father's intentions. One day in late May, Dad and I did what we did every morning. We ate breakfast at the same oak kitchen table we'd always had since I could remember, the table that claimed my first lost tooth at age four when my brother Jack pushed me into it. I always opened my morning with a bowl of Frosted Mini-Wheats while my father ate cereal from a bowl he had poured the night before. He lived for the taste of stuff like Mueslix and Grape-Nuts soaked to saturation with the milk the cereal ingested throughout the night in the fridge. I tried to do the same thing briefly but never understood the allure.

"Jared," my father asked me one morning, "what should we do this summer?" Dad stared over the top of the newspaper at me as his words reached me, peering over his glasses and down his nose.

"Dad, you ask this every year. Usually Jack and I say New York or Boston, someplace with a lot to do and see, and we go. And who can forget the yearly trip to the Boat Graveyard. This year, I think we should do what you would like."

"Wow, Pickle, I never thought you would say that." Dad always called me Pickle for some unknown reason. I never knew how the name stuck or why it started. I always answered to it, so it never bothered me. "Maybe we should ask Jack."

"No, Dad, I think we should do what you would like. In fact, I'd like to go on one of your little digs. I know it would be fun."

"Tell you what, Jared. How about we take some of you and Jack's friends with us this time? You know, make it sort of a celebration of you kids graduating. That is, if Jack does graduate."

"Sounds cool. I'll talk with them as soon as I see them today. I'm sure some people would like to go."

"Great." Anybody who knew Seamus McCracken knew that the conversation ended when he started using one word sentences. Any further talk after that was pointless.

I left the dining room and bounded up the stairs to collect my school books from my room. The prospects of venturing out with Dad on one of his expeditions appealed to me like a beautiful woman. The sheer joy Dad would no doubt experience watching his two sons showing interest in his work could not be measured by conventional scales or charts. The hair on my neck stood on end at the thought of finding some ancient artifact, a trinket linked to the first people to walk these shores or a relic of the past. The early morning waking coma most teens wander with every day did not plague me on that occasion.

The closer I got to school, the tougher it was for me to contain my excitement. Jack sat in the back of the Ford Windstar, following his normal daily ritual of resting his eyes in the back. At least this day he refrained from curling up in the cargo bay.

"See you after school, boys," Dad pronounced as we arrived at Brandh High.

"Later, Dad," I replied. "I'll have an answer from everyone by the end of the day."

Dad drove away in the van, leaving Jack and me on a sidewalk leading through a courtyard decorated with a statue of a snarling black bear raised on its haunches. We began walking toward the front door of the school when Jack grabbed my arm.

"An answer to what?" he asked.

"Let me tell you about Dad's idea for our summer trip…" I began as we pushed through a set of double doors and walked into the school.

CHAPTER 3

Besides me, there would be four of us going on the trip, at least four of us that I knew about. My father was fifty-three at the time and was showing signs of growing old fast. His eyesight, always a bone of contention with him, had gotten worse over the previous six months, particularly in his right eye. Dad's optometrist in Bangor, Dr. Herndon, discovered the onset of glaucoma during Dad's last visit. Dad continued to wear his normal glasses, but his right eye constantly bothered him, causing him to suffer from occasional headaches and other minor inconveniences. He rubbed his eyes a lot and preferred for Jack or me to drive whenever we were available.

He worked as a professor at the University of Maine, using his background in archaeology to teach world cultures. Dad never missed a day of work. "It's what I do so it's where I be," he would always say when someone would ask him why he would fight against any illness to maintain his perfect attendance. He figured he led by example, showing his students that he cared enough to be there every day and therefore they should try to be there for him as well.

I always felt I owed Dad since birth. When I was born there were complications. Dad's first wife, my mother the former Jill Thorburn, hemorrhaged when I crowned, causing irreparable internal bleeding. The doctors tried to save her, but nothing kept her from going to God. So as an infant I grew up with one parent. I felt totally responsible for costing Dad his true love.

Dad remarried shortly after I turned two. I'd heard stories from Aunt Sheila about how cute I was as the ring bearer at that wedding.

Dad married Kara Clemons, the town librarian. He often told the story of how he remembered the first time he met Kara, how her shimmering blond hair and melting green eyes combined to take his hurt away. Usually, the story turned into a series of one word sentences when I prodded Dad for more elaboration.

That divorce brought me my stepbrother Jack. Jack came to us when Kara married Dad and stayed after the custody battle. He was nearly the same age as me, only about seven months my junior. In fact, he and I shared most of the same classes, with the exceptions of my advanced courses and his remedial classes. Jack chose not to work hard, ironically the same path Kara's next husband the shop steward took. He preferred the low-key lifestyle, skating by in class and skirting under the law's radar with his occasional drinking.

I did love my brother Jack, I just didn't agree with how he carried himself. I knew he could have done better but he didn't apply himself or try to be a bigger part of our family. He suffered from that short man's disease, angry that he stood only five foot eight, and as a result he often took on the pit bull mentality, tenaciously chewing away at people until he wore them down and got his way. Psychologists often referred to his situation as an inferiority complex. I thought he was just generally pissed off at the world and me in particular.

Of course, Jack obviously had redeeming qualities. You needed to look no further than his girlfriend, Erin Lomansky. Erin lived with her mother, a widower thanks to friendly fire in the Gulf War. Erin saw something in Jack that most of us couldn't see, a sense of love for someone else. Erin often got compared to Drew Barrymore as far as looks, build, and personality go, but I always countered with that Natalie girl from the Dixie Chicks, back before she started butchering her hair and wearing the garish outfits. I knew why Jack went out with Erin, because I liked her too. That often happened when there was only one girl in a group.

DOME OF THE ROCK

Actually, comparing Erin to any other person would be unfair. I believed this because in my mind, Erin had no equal. There was no other person like her. No one carried the class, charm, sex appeal, wit, intelligence, beauty, humor, and compassion better in a five foot six, one hundred twenty pound, strawberry blonde package than she did, and nobody could ever be asked to try. Putting pressure to excel in that way on any one person was a burden that no person could dare even think of matching.

I'd known Erin longer than Jack. She and I grew up together from a young age, before kindergarten or even before Dad met Kara. Erin and I spent summers swimming in Brandh Lake, autumns gorging ourselves on blueberries while hired hands harvested them, and winters sliding down King George Hill on our sleds. When she broke her arm at six falling out of a tree, I carried her to our house. When I participated in the regional finals of the Punt, Pass, and Kick contest, she served as my unofficial coach. Our friendship blossomed further as she continued to date my stepbrother Jack.

The other one I invited was Ben Hunter. Choosing Ben was an easy choice. He loved the outdoors. Ben's cousins were the Harsteins, the same Harsteins who owned the chain of hotels up and down the east coast, those same ones who bought into the Patriots. Ben came from money, and he used his resources to buy outdoor equipment and all sorts of gadgets. He was the first person I knew who owned a DVD player, as well as the only person I knew who had climbed Mount Katahdin.

There's one more thing about Ben. Most of his friends called him by another name.

"Hey Dewey" always served to grab his attention. We called him Dewey because he never shut up about the former Red Sox outfielder Dwight Evans. Almost weekly he'd approach us with some new obscure statistic or news on the latest with the right fielder of our youth. I still remembered clearly the time we visited Fenway

Park and Ben nearly collapsed when he got Mr. Evans' autograph. He didn't care that Dwight coached and didn't play by that time. To an eight year old, meeting the greatest athlete in one's eyes can only be topped by kidnapping Santa Claus and holding him for toy ransom. Ben kept that signed napkin in his locker at school, the centerpiece in his shrine to his deity.

Each of us wanted to spend the weekend together on Dad's adventure. I was assuming everything in that statement of course, but I believed that each individual would have backed out at the slightest hint of a doubt. I knew each of us shared the same idea, the notion that this trip represented one last chance at holding on to our youth and keeping the unstoppable crew from fading away.

Our group of voyagers set, the only thing left to do was to wait for the inevitable, the day when our adventure would begin.

CHAPTER 4

None of us knew what to expect as we filed into the den that evening, a mere two weeks before our graduation. Dad held all the cards. He alone knew what he wanted to achieve; the rest of us went to the meeting hoping for answers and the prospect of a great time together.

"Thanks for coming, my children."

"What do you have in mind for us, Dad?"

Dad sat in a deep leather chair behind his grand oak desk. The rest of us pushed stools and chairs from other rooms on the second story of the house into a semi-circle around him. Ben and I both carried spiral notebooks and pens. Erin tussled with Jack, trying unsuccessfully to keep him from nibbling softly on her neck.

Dad's office in the den usually spooked those new to the house. The wall to the right of Dad's ridiculously large, high desk was, in actuality, a series of shelves. Each row carried the heavy burden of books upon books. Textbooks, notebooks, journals, pages wrapped together in their makeshift spines with dirty twine, and any other form of literature adorned these shelves. According to Dad, he had read each and every one of the texts on his shelves, no matter how obscure the text in question. The light in the study stayed low at all times, even during a brilliantly sunny day. The one window in the room, a small half circle of glass, faced away from both the rising and setting sun. Completing the ambiance of this room, a twisted, gnarled potted tree drooped in the corner opposite the only entrance. I'd caught Dad talking to that tree on more than one occasion, usually with his back to the entryway and his hands clasped behind him. Sometimes, at night, I swore that tree reached for me as I stumbled past it, through the darkness from my room to the bathroom. Simply put, this office of Dad's reminded most people of the spooky library of a Dr. Frankenstein or some other mad scientist.

"You all know Jared brought you here for a reason." Dad sipped from a glass of water as he began to speak. "First, congratulations to each of you. Graduating from high school, although not what it once was, is still a great accomplishment."

"If I graduate," Jared replied. Dad's raised palm helped to control our giggling.

"Nevertheless, I'm happy all of you decided to join me for my next expedition." He opened a drawer to his left and produced a series of documents from within it.

"Expedition?" Ben and I both asked in unison.

"Yes," Dad replied. "Pickle, would you be so kind as to pass these around the room?"

He handed me four copies of a stapled packet. Each packet was identical, complete with a cover page of canary yellow paper, nothing printed on it. The back cover was also the same yellow color. I passed one to each of my three fellow teenagers as Dad continued.

"This manifest explains what we plan to do. Gentlemen, and lady, I want to attempt to find an ancient site, here on our coast, a site of untold potential for life. I want to find the site of Ragnarok."

"Oh, here we go," Jack cackled.

"Shut up," Erin grunted, elbowing him in the ribs.

"If you would turn to the second page in your manifests and follow along please." Following Dad's instructions, we all leafed through the dossier to the second page. The first page showed a crude map, hand drawn, with a makeshift compass in the margin. The second page carried the heading "Ulric Johannsen" at the top.

"Most scholars believe that the idea of a battlefield of the gods here on Earth is preposterous. They scoff at the idea of such a thing, the idea that tangible proof of the afterlife can exist among us. They don't think that this place I speak of is out there. I happen to think differently.

"The gentleman whose name is at the top of the page, Ulric Johannsen, is the man whom I believe held the key. I've researched his life and find no evidence that would cause me not to trust his word. Ulric was born in Viking territories sometime around 896 A.D. and undertook his first voyage to the New World aboard a Viking ship around the year 914."

"What's this got to do with us?" Jack asked.

"Shut up," Ben responded.

"To continue," Dad said, "the remarkable thing about Ulric Johannsen was his determination." As he continued to speak, Dad rose from his leather chair and approached the bookcase. "After seeing what he did during his first trip to our shores, he returned to the Scandinavian hinterlands and taught himself to write, albeit at a limited level."

"Like Jack," I laughed.

"Shut up," Jack replied.

Dad scanned the second shelf from the ceiling for a moment, until his eyes fell on a tattered bundle pushed among the other books. He carefully pulled the misshapen beast from the shelf, walked with it between his sure hands to his desk, and returned to the seated position.

"When Ulric made his second journey across the sea, sometime around 920, he brought with him this item."

We all inched forward to view the so-called book of Dad's. The cover of this text was nothing more than a thick piece of tree bark. Flakes of it fell off the front as Dad lifted the cover and turned it to expose the interior. The pages, covered with a series of indecipherable scribbles, were animal hides. This flimsy journal to the past had no business still surviving.

"This thing smells," Jack said.

"Shut up!" Erin, Ben, and I all yelled.

"In this volume, Ulric Johannsen details what he saw on his trip to what he called The Land Beyond The Sun. He describes an island where a great gate stood. The shimmer of this gate served as a beacon that drowned out all other light on the horizon. Outside this gate, as Ulric describes it, he saw the allfather Odin's most trusted guardians, Hugin and Munin, a pair of ferocious wolves, waiting for their master to join them. Ulric writes that this gate is the gate to Valhalla, the hall of the slain, our heaven.

"Ulric died shortly thereafter, and this writing remained hidden deep within a village in England until discovered in the late nineteenth century. It remained in a book shop until 1937, when my father found it and bought the book for twelve pounds. A text of this importance would be a steal at a million times the price."

"We should sell it on eBay," Jack declared.

"As Jack and Jared both know, my father explored the European countryside much of his life. What my father did was search for fame and fortune. He believed that the Ragnarok site lied somewhere in the islands off the coast of Ireland."

"Why was that?" Ben asked.

"The description of the Land Beyond The Sun led him to think that it had to be to the west. Ulric talked of the long journey across the cruel sea to the outcroppings on the end of the world. My father studied the common routes possible and came up with the logical solution of searching in these islands.

"Only problem was, these islands didn't match up with the description. One thing I haven't told you yet is what happened to the island. The way Ulric Johannsen describes it, the island suffered a terrible catastrophe as he watched. The interior peak of the island caved in upon itself and toppled into the ocean, leaving less than half of the mountain itself intact. He watched the gate disappear on the back of the plateau that made the top of this great mountain. He stated in his writing that it never disintegrated, it merely fell intact into the center of the crater left behind, not to be seen again until the proper time and only by the truly worthy."

"Sounds cool," I said. I received nods of agreement from my friends in attendance.

"My father bounced around the smaller islands in the British isles, starting in the strait between England and Ireland. He soon moved his search to those islands along the western border of Ireland, searching island by island with no luck. After years of trying, he nearly gave up when he heard of a volcanic eruption on Iceland. Knowing that the Vikings had used Iceland as a port in later times, my father went there to explore the possibility. Unfortunately for him, he never returned from that mission, succumbing to pneumonia in 1970."

Ben raised his hand before speaking. "If you don't mind me asking...why do you think this place does exist? And...if you do...where is it?"

"Good question. Like I said, I find no information to contradict Ulric Johannsen's writings. His words just seem to seep the pages with the truth. Also, many pieces of folklore have been created out of facts of the world around us. The area he describes in his writing is consistent with volcanic activity of the time period."

"And to answer your second question, please turn to the maps on the first page."

We leafed over to the map page in our respective packets. The map shown was an overhead view of an island, drawn to scale as best a person with the onset of glaucoma could create. Crude notes decorated various points on the map, as did approximate heights and distances.

"I created this map based on the original drawing in Ulric's journal. He gave heights and distances like I have here. His drawing wasn't a view from above like this, but based on the scale of his drawing I filled in the gaps. As you can see, there is a jagged peak rising to the eastern side of the island in question. Debris litters the crater below, but the bulk of the mountain fell into the sea, here to the north and to the northwest. The western end of the island is an open space, allowing entrance into the lava dome itself."

"Lava dome?" Erin asked.

"Don't worry, my dear child. A lava dome is merely the expansion below the surface in an active volcano that hasn't erupted again. Eventually, the magma below the surface causes enough stress on the cooled rock above it to escape. The name shouldn't frighten you. A lava dome isn't any more harmful than a glacier in winter."

"You should fear Jack more," I added. Dad's raised hand silenced us once more.

"One more important feature to the island. Here, near the summit of the high east side, there's a boulder sitting by itself. According to Ulric, when the island stopped blowing up, he spotted this rock at the top of the peak. He describes the rock as being the head of an enormous snake."

A lightning flash went off inside my head. "Dad, you don't mean..."

"Yes, Pickle, I do. Kids, after an exhaustive study, I think I know where this island is. Oh, it is to the west of the Viking homeland. My father just didn't think to look far enough to the west. The island we will visit after your graduation, with your consent of course, is Baffert Island."

CHAPTER 5

The next two weeks blurred by. We all prepared for our trip, but only when preparations for graduation didn't come first. Jack drank too much whiskey before prom and got himself and Erin thrown out of the affair. I went with Rebecca Shannon, a sweet redhead who doubled as my study partner in AP English. She and I were too different, and during the night our incompatibility reared its ugly head. I liked her, but liking someone doesn't always pan out into anything more. Such was my way with Rebecca.

Finals proved too easy, and soon the day came for us to receive our diplomas. Our ceremony took place in the field outside the school. The stage rested toward the back of the field, near the tree line. The bleachers sufficed to provide enough seating capacity for those in attendance. Those of us graduating nervously awaited our diplomas from our spots in the auditorium's folding chairs, placed in rows of eight on the grass in front of the stage. I felt bad for poor Greta Van der Houton, the one person who occupied the fifth and last row by herself. Jack, Erin, Ben, and I sat side by side together in the second row, on the right end. Yes, Jack somehow earned his ticket out of high school with the rest of us, just under the wire.

Headmaster Higgins barely contained his false enthusiasm for our class. "This group of students is not only the largest class we've ever produced, but also the brightest." I knew the second part was a lie since he had the line as a part of his speech every year, like that sentence appeared somewhere in his contract as a necessity.

Most of that ceremony dragged on, to the point where I caught myself nearly dozing off a couple of separate times. Jack's eyes were closed so he was in worse shape. I backhanded him in the chest to jar him awake as Dad took the stage with the keynote speech.

"My young ones, never forget what you've accomplished. You represent the bright future of life, the wonderful results of hard work and determination. You young ladies and gentlemen sitting before me are each equally great. I am proud of each of you.

"Now, as your new lives begin, never forget what your time here meant to you. Never forget what this place was to you. Remember the good times, cherish the fact that you survived the rough patches, and always keep the thoughts of your time here in your mind and the fondness of the time here in your hearts. Live your lives like the noble black bear that each of you was for the past four years.

"As you go out into the world around you, as you make the best for yourselves, remember this simple reminder. Each of us has a story. Live yours."

I think I stood first, but it wasn't a race for me. Every person at that ceremony, both in the graduating class and in the bleachers, rose to their feet and clapped. Soon enough, people in Dad's audience whooped and hooted in response to his great words. We calmed as Dad raised his palm and asked for attention.

"So, before we officially graduate each of you, I must ask for you to do me one favor. My Black Bears, you must convince me you are ready. Are you ready Black Bears?"

The concussive blast of our emphatic "Yes!" moved Dad from the microphone.

"Then let me hear it!"

With that, all thirty-three of us dove into the words to the fight song.

"We are the Black Bears from the shores of the Brandh,
Filled with nobility,

DOME OF THE ROCK

Always with pride through the countryside,
We walk with a glide, strive to survive,
Soon when you come up against one of our den,
Know that's it's best to flee,
Cause we'll Fight! Claw! Scratch! To the top!
To vic…tor…y!"

With that, the crowd erupted into cheers. Some of us started jumping up and down. Jack slapped me on the chest, and I gave him a good playful push in kind. Mortarboards filled the air and littered the landscape. The graduating class of Brandh High School was a mob scene of joy as we all celebrated the final moment of our scholastic time together.

Dad met us at the end of the festivities. "Congratulations, my children," he beamed. He seemed more pleased for us than we were.

"Thanks, Dr. McCracken," Ben and Erin replied as Jack and I rushed to hug him. Jack let go first and bounded off to find his mother.

"Are you kids ready for our trip?" Dad rubbed his eye under his glasses as he asked.

"We sure are." I smiled as I replied to him. My honor cords began to twist around themselves, so I worked to untangle them before they constricted around my windpipe.

"Dr. McCracken," Ben said, "I have a question for you."

"Yes, son?"

"I was wondering…would there be…any…climbing on this trip?"

"Ben, you can count on it."

Ben grinned deeply with the assurance from Dad. "Great! I'll bring my stuff."

"I'd have it no other way."

I couldn't hold in my own joy for the occasion any longer. I grabbed Dad in an embrace once more, squeezed him tight, and kissed him on the cheek. Dad hugged me in return, refusing to let go until I did so first.

As I looked over his shoulder, I noticed Jack, standing by himself near the bleachers. He strained his eyes, looking around the field, searching for something that he couldn't seem to find. His eyes wandered through the small groups that littered the field, surveying the faces and trying in vain to find one person standing alone, a person he couldn't uncover.

Jack slowly walked back to the group. He pecked Erin on the cheek and looked at Dad.

"Dad," he asked, "where's Mom?"

"Didn't you call her, son?"

Jack took a deep breath before speaking again. I could tell he was reaching his boiling point. "No," he breathed in, "you were supposed to call her."

"No, Jack," Dad replied, "I told you to invite her. You know she doesn't like talking to me."

Jack thrust his hands under his gown and into his pockets. "No, you were supposed to invite her. Now she's not here. Perfect!"

Jack turned and rushed away from our group, huffing to the bleachers. He flopped down on the first riser and slapped it with his open right palm.

"Son, wait," Dad pleaded, but Jack merely waved him away. Jack stood, looked at us for a moment, and began to walk home. He skipped his mortarboard across the ground, leaving it to rest against a tree.

CHAPTER 6

"Jack, would you come on already?"

I yelled from my room to his, waiting for him to respond. As I asked for his answer, I made my final preparations for the evening. I checked my hair, making sure each fine brown strand laid down properly on my scalp. I was never blessed with great hair, more like a finely kept nest of follicles that quietly stayed just on the fringes of high fashion. I'd gone to the Caesar cut early in my senior year, a cut that required me to actually pay attention to it *every day*. Talk about a pain.

I pulled on my favorite coat, my peacoat that Grampy Killington had given me a couple years before. It was his jacket from when he served in the Navy in World War II, a nice warm jacket that Jack constantly showed envy of. All Grampy gave him was a pocket watch from the same time, a watch that Jack kept amid the clutter on top of his dresser.

"Jack?" I asked again as I wandered down the hall, past Dad's study, and to his door, across the hall from the bathroom. Jack sat on the bed with the lights out. Darkness approached outside, but it was still light enough out to see into his room. Jack sat on the bed alone, save for a stack of letters that surrounded him. His yearbook also lay on the bed, resting comfortably on top of his discarded gown.

"Jack, you ready for tonight?"

He looked up, hearing me for the first time. "Yeah," he replied, slowly and quietly, "I'm ready."

"You know Dad's not to blame."

"Sure." Jack rose from his bed and rushed past me and down the hall. We bounded down the stairs and were nearly out the door before Dad stopped us. "Now you two be careful tonight," he said. He paused for a moment, thrusting his hands into his pockets. Producing some cash, he asked us, "Do you need any money?"

"No, Dad," I said.

"Thanks, Pops," Jack countered, grabbing the full wad from Dad before Dad produced an offer. Jack threw open the door as I reassured Dad that we'd be fine.

* * *

"I can't wait for Bar Harbor," Erin squealed. She and Jack rode in the back seat of the Windstar, giggling occasionally as they swiped a kiss from each other. Ben and I occupied the front of the vehicle, me behind the wheel.

"Why wait?" Jack replied. He removed a flask from his coat pocket, uncapped the lid, and lifted the small bottle to his lips. Gulping deeply, Jack finished his drink with a refreshed exhalation. He offered the flask to Erin, who sipped lightly from it.

"Damn, that burns," she hissed through the fire in her throat.

"Shit is good," Jack replied. He drank again, then offered the flask to Ben and me up front. I declined, Ben sipped lightly, and Jack gulped down another dose. "Hey, turn this shit up," he ordered, and we obliged by turning the volume of the radio up slightly, letting some fast, guitar driven country hoe-down tune permeate every corner of the cabin.

"I hope there's hotties at this party," Jack proclaimed to the car as we turned the corner into Bar Harbor.

Erin nudged him in the ribs. "You're already with a hottie," she replied.

Jack laughed. "Oh yeah. That's right." He sipped from his flask again. "Hey, stop up ahead."

"Why?" I asked.

"You do want to get fucked up, right?"

I lied to him. "A little, yeah."

"Then pull over here. This place'll sell to me."

I pulled into a parking lot in front of the first grocery store I saw. Jack had the sliding door open before I even stopped the van.

"Just leave it running," he said. "I'll be fast."

"Jack, no," Erin pleaded, but her concerns fell short of Jack's ears. He bounded into the store, a slight drunken limp in his step.

"What's he got planned?" I asked her, but she just shook her head in the back seat.

I could see him inside the store as he wandered over to the beverage aisle. I saw him hit on a college aged girl, no doubt using his favorite opening line: "Hey, let's fuck." She exited, obviously appalled by such an offer. Jack always contended that someday that line would actually work. I never understood how Erin put up with that kind of confidence.

Jack emerged from the cooler aisle with a suitcase of beer under his left arm. He wandered slowly toward the magazine rack, mere feet from the front entrance to the store. His Red Sox hat was pulled low over his eyes, and I finally figured out what was coming next. I slipped the van into reverse, dimmed the headlights, and backed away from the front of the building. Shifting into drive and angling the Windstar toward the street, I kept one eye on Jack as he studied the magazines. More accurately, he studied the store personnel over the top of the magazine he pretended to look through. Two older women worked the check stands, paying attention to the customers that had started to form lines by their respective counters. Jack dropped the magazine, picked up the suitcase of beer, and took one small step.

"Keep that door open," I sighed. We'd be getting drunk now for sure. Jack flashed one quick glance to the two checkers, waited for a lady with a cart to approach, and ran out as she triggered the electronic door. Jack carried the beer like a fullback, tucking it against his body with both arms so as not to fumble the precious contents. He yelled out "Go! GO!" as he neared the van. As he did so, he started to stumble over his own feet. Not one of those sad stumbles a young girl often suffers, but rather the kind of comical drunken stumble where the body of the victim takes about ten steps to go down. Jack's momentum started to carry him over as he reached the van. Luckily for him, I waited for him to hit the van's interior before I sped off. I could have created the damn funniest scene ever had I moved the van and allowed him to slam face first into the quarter panel. He half fell, half dove headfirst into the van as I peeled the tires and entered the safety of Friday evening Bar Harbor traffic. An oncoming Jeep flashed their brights, reminding me to turn the headlights back on. Jack laughed hysterically on the floor in the back of the van.

"You're a damn fool," I remarked as Erin slammed the sliding door shut.

"Maybe so," Jack heaved between breaths, "but I'm also going to get fucked up tonight!" He tore into the cardboard packaging, quickly producing a can of golden ale from the box. He handed one to Erin, one to Ben, and cracked open his first of many. I focused on the road before us, the constantly changing collection of license plates from different states that surrounded us at all times.

We slowly crept through Bar Harbor, our progress choked off by the sizable amount of traffic. Bar Harbor itself wasn't such a large place, but the allure of this seaside port came from the town's time warp feel. Bar Harbor only needed to disallow paved roads to return to the late eighteenth century, with nearly every building maintaining the same charm they no doubt held during the dawning of the United States itself. From the post office to the bike shop, every building in Bar Harbor carried the same rustic personality of its long since discarded style of erection. I wasn't exactly sure what you'd call this type of design, but I'd heard it called colonial and Victorian interchangeably by both locals and tourists alike. Each structure had the same high archways, elaborate porches, and quaint wooden beams. As an added bonus, the town looked out over the Atlantic Ocean, completing the romantic feel for many couples in love.

The tourist season seemed to be in full effect, judging by the series of vehicles that surrounded us. Cars from Massachusetts, New Hampshire, and Vermont always traveled the main road during the summer months. Transportation from Connecticut, New York, Rhode Island, and New Jersey was not uncommon. I'd seen cars from as far away as Oregon in Bar Harbor at times, people who undoubtedly wanted to return to a simpler time and didn't mind being taken advantage of financially for their wishes.

We turned right when we reached the wharf, following the road through the tourist attractions and out toward the residential area. Most visitors to Bar Harbor probably didn't realize that this was a town and not some historical resort like Williamsburg, Virginia. Actual people led their lives in Bar Harbor, and when the flocks of vacationers would leave others remained to continue their daily lives. They did so in the secrecy of their secluded community, away from the gawking glaze of the glassy-eyed rubes that migrated every summer to their favorite seaside spot.

"Are we there yet?" I asked, slowly creeping up a side street.

"Wait. Um, yeah, right…there." Jack thrust his hand forward from the back seat, pointing his left index finger past my ear and to a cottage set back from the street. A picket fence ringed the yard, a fence covered in moss in places and in terrible need of a paint job. A sidewalk led from an opening in the fence to the base of a porch, much like my house except dirtier. Automobiles were parked on both sides of the street, down the block in both directions. We crawled down the road about a block and parked the Windstar in the first available space we encountered.

"This is it?" I asked as I exited the van. The house didn't look dilapidated, just haunted.

"You betcha," Jack replied, tucking the suitcase of beer under his arm. "Come on, this'll kick ass."

We wandered up to the porch, each of us cracking open a can in the shadows. As we began to step up to the front door, the door flew open and a man stumbled to the railing. He doubled over at the rail and coughed deeply, immediately spewing fluid to the lawn beneath him.

"Nice to meet you," I greeted, extending my hand. He looked up at me, smiled a vomit grin, and hurled again.

We entered the house and within a second were greeted by the stench of spilled alcohol. The front room, which took up about half of the lower floor, was wall to wall teens. I knew many of these people by sight but not everyone. It seemed as though about half of our graduating class had made it to this secret location. Kids from other schools also filled the room, pounding beers, gulping concoctions, or sipping freely from the bottle. Girls hung on guys, girls hung on girls, and girls hung on furniture. Other boys grouped together in packs throughout the room, making fun of each other in the social version of the pissing contest.

Jack scrambled off in one direction, tugging Erin with him as he carried the suitcase of beer. He turned and tossed me a beer over his shoulder. I caught it before it smashed into Brandy Carrigan's nose, which would have been tragic if she wasn't already a troll. Ben and I wandered over to the far end of the room, greeting those we knew and nodding to those who recognized us only as the ones drinking the coldest beer.

* * *

"Hey, Jared." I heard my name come from a seductive voice behind me. I turned to find the source of the greeting. I'd been at this party an hour, but up until then I'd managed to avoid the girl who now wanted my attention.

"Hey, Molly," I sighed, knowing that my best efforts to avoid Molly had been for naught.

Molly Simmons was better known throughout the county as Mattressback, because, well…there were rumors. She stood head and shoulders ahead of the other girls when it came to developing physically, socially, and sexually. For some odd reason, her large teal eyes fell upon me that spring. Maybe it was the thrill of the hunt, maybe she needed a challenge, or maybe she suffered from such low esteem that she thought bedding me would earn my respect. Whatever the reason, I could see that she figured that this night provided the best chance to complete her mission.

"Didn't think you were going to make it," she cooed to me. I couldn't help but admit to myself that she did look pretty good that evening. She wore an off-white sleeveless top and a red lacy bra underneath that showed through in a subtle tease. She definitely brought the goods up top, stretching that sleeveless blouse to the limits. Her tight midriff, complete with downright sexy naval piercing, exposed itself from the bottom of the shirt. She wore a black pleated skirt and black shoes, for all I knew. I didn't spend much time looking at her feet. I found it hard to get past the upper body, but I did know her black skirt didn't cover a whole heck of a lot either. She looked classy, not like a hooker, but she definitely was dressed for action. She wore her chestnut hair down that evening, and it played in the space around her face, framing her brilliant teal eyes, narrow nose, and full lips.

"Wasn't going to miss it," I said in a raised voice, trying to talk to her over the noise around us, the dozens of discussions and thumping music.

Ben stood beside me, sipping from a beer, one I had no idea where he got from. Jack had disappeared into another part of the house, the neighborhood, the state for all I knew. I hadn't seen him since we arrived over an hour before. He and Erin, his hostage, shared this party with us in logistics only, although I had seen her briefly earlier, a frantic look in her eye as she wandered alone through the crowd.

"I saw you came in the van," Molly purred. "Maybe I'll see you out there later."

"Guaranteed," I replied. "I'll need to leave in it."

Molly tossed her head back as she laughed. She clutched her right hand to her chest as she laughed, almost like she wanted to make sure I knew that she possessed two of the finest breasts ever to occupy New England. I recognized this fact quite clearly.

She reached over to me and touched my cheek with her right hand. "Maybe I can leave with you tonight," she whispered in my ear as she pulled me closer to her. She pressed her lips to mine for a moment then pulled away, running her hand from my cheek down my chest to my waist before relinquishing contact. She flipped her hair as she turned on her toe and let her breasts lead her to another part of the house.

"Dewey?" I asked Ben.

"Yes, Jared?"

"Don't let that happen. Got it?"

"You damn right I won't. You heard what happened to Walt?"

"Yep. I didn't know someone could do that to themselves."

As Ben and I laughed together, Erin crashed through the crowd in a panic.

"Come quick, guys," she pleaded.

"What's up?" I asked, stepping toward her as I engaged her.

"Jack's going after Troy Utley."

"Ah, shit," I groaned, and the three of us frantically started pushing our way through the crowd.

Erin led us through the rear of the house into a courtyard out back. When we got there, we found a crowd gathering. In the center, on the ground, Jack and Troy Utley tussled in an angry grapple.

Troy lived in Hampstead, not far from us. He hated Jack ever since the night he found Jack feeling up his former girlfriend Cheryl Watkins junior year at Homecoming. Neither boy had the upper hand in this bout as they rolled around on the moist grass, trading blows to each other's sides.

"Jack talk trash again?" I asked Erin as we reached the inner circle. She nodded back through her forlorn expression.

"Come on, Dewey," I pleaded.

Ben and I jumped into the fight. I yanked Jack from the scrum and Ben shadowed Troy, keeping his body between Troy and Jack. The combatants traded insults, stringing together words only sailors and drunks would dare try to piece into sentences. Troy and Jack wagged fingers at each other and generally tried to act tough in front of the crowd. Ben managed to calm Troy, offering our remaining stash of beer, which for some reason had dwindled down to about four cans after only an hour and a half. I pulled Jack around to the side of the house.

"What the hell was that?" I screamed. I held Jack by the shoulders, shaking him with my arms.

"He fucking started it," Jack snarled. "Sorry bitch."

"I don't care," I growled. "This is bullshit!"

I let go of Jack and tried to take a deep breath. The anger caused me by my embarrassment of a brother constricted my chest. I continued heaving in air, but the fire inside me wouldn't allow me to calm down. Jack paced in the darkness.

"Every time," I hissed. "Every time!"

Jack turned toward the house, reared back, and kicked the outer wall with his boot. I knew that hurt like a son of a bitch, but Jack never flinched or limped. He was so full of liquor he probably would never remember kicking the structure.

Erin and Ben found us on the side of the house. "We should go," said Ben.

"Yeah," Erin agreed.

"Dammit!" Jack rushed through pursed lips. He let his clenched fists subside, breathed in deeply, and reluctantly followed the rest of us around the house to the front yard.

We reached the opening in the picket fence when I heard footsteps behind us.

"Don't leave," Molly called out, bounding down the steps in a flurry of cleavage.

"Sorry Matt…I mean Molly. Jack's had too much. I need to take him home."

"Yeah, so he can spank it," Jack retorted. He chuckled to himself.

"Can't I go with you?" The night chill influenced the contents of her shirt in a rather stimulating way. My eyes widened in the splendor of the scene.

"I'm sorry," I responded. "We're going to need to lay Jack down in the back. He'll want to sleep this off."

"Damn." Molly slid her hands up her hips before placing them on her own ass. "Can I call you then?"

"Uh…sure," I stammered.

"What's your number?" Molly stumbled forward a step. The scent of cranberries and vodka entered my nostrils.

"Seven six five, four three, two one."

"Same area code as mine?"

"Yeah Molly, same area code. Talk to you tomorrow." I draped Jack's right arm over my left shoulder and helped walk him to the van. Molly remained stationary just outside the fence, watching as our crew of four disappeared into the darkness. I caught one final glimpse of her reentering the party before I closed the van door and turned the key in the ignition.

I didn't hear from Molly the next day.

CHAPTER 7

"You guys ready?"

"Yeah, Dad. Be right down."

I stuffed one more sweatshirt into my duffel bag and closed my bedroom door behind me. Jack emerged from his room at the same time with a backpack over his shoulder and a smaller bag in his left hand. Both of us wore more clothes than necessary for the June day. Jack had a sweatshirt tied around his waist, and I wore a windbreaker over the top of my long sleeved T-shirt. As we reached the top landing of the stairs, Jack tossed the smaller bag with an underhand motion to the floor below. The bag skidded to a halt against a pair of sleeping bags.

"This should be good," he complained, like always.

"Shut up, Jack," I countered, nudging him down the stairs to the front passage.

Dad peered through the contents of his luggage while standing in the passageway. The items he carried outnumbered what Jack and I packed in both size and weight. I witnessed a series of instruments drop into his backpack and charts into his shoulder satchel. He worked over his baggage with the swiftness and precision of a surgeon, following a mental checklist and almost instantly itemizing his necessities. He looked up from his bags as he zipped them up.

"You guys all packed?" he asked.

"Yes," Jack replied. "Two clean pairs of underpants and everything."

"Thank God," I laughed.

"Great. Go ahead and load the van. I just need to make a quick couple of phone calls and we'll be on our way." Dad kept his head down the entire time he spoke to us.

With that, Jack and I carried the bags out to the van.

We carefully placed the baggage into the rear compartment of the Windstar. I tried to push everything toward the outer walls of the compartment, while Jack preferred the method of tossing stuff in and letting it stay wherever it rested. We closed the tailgate and loaded into the van as Dad emerged from the house, locking the door before approaching.

"We're all set then, children," he said, handing me the keys. "Jack, please ride in the back so I can navigate."

"Yes sir," Jack shouted. He then clicked his heels together and saluted.

We all climbed into the van, and with a turn of the key in the ignition switch, left our home behind.

* * *

"Forget anything, Dewey?" Jack asked Ben from the back of the van. "Jesus."

"It can never hurt to be prepared, Jack. You know, Dwight Evans carried a mitt for the outfield and first base with him at all times."

"Good for him. I bet he never had to lug a million pounds of shit for Jim Rice."

Ben and Erin both sat in the back seat of the Windstar, Ben nearest the sliding door and Erin with her head on Jack's right shoulder. Jack's left shoulder pressed against the window.

"Don't mind him, son," Dad answered. "I trust you brought what you wanted."

"Yes sir, Dr. McCracken," Ben replied. "I brought all my climbing equipment for this trip."

"Good. I think it will come in handy. It's likely we'll need to climb the eastern face of the mountain to get a look at the area there."

"Climbing?" Jack muttered gruffly. "I didn't sign up for that."

I flashed a glance back in the rear view mirror at Erin. She looked at Jack for a second, caught my gaze in the corner of her eye, looked forward at my reflection, and smiled simultaneously with me.

"Okay son, we need to turn here." Dad pointed to two tire ruts that cut into the woods on the right edge of the highway, just past a single mailbox positioned atop a stump. I slowed and turned the Windstar down this dirt trail. Low hanging trees reached down at the van, but just couldn't quite grab us. We bumped along for a quarter mile or so then came to a clearing. At the far end of this clearing, ringed by dense trees, a small mobile trailer awaited us.

"This it, Dad?" I asked.

"Yes, Pickle."

"What a shithole," Jack chuckled. Erin smacked him on the chest as she raised her head from his shoulder.

I stopped the van in front of the trailer as a gentleman exited the structure. He wore a full beard, pockmarked with salt-and-pepper patches throughout. His thick hair covered his ears and flowed back from his forehead to the middle of his neck. He didn't carry much weight on his tall frame, easily more than six foot three, as his body stretched almost featureless from his clavicle to his metatarsal. He bounded down from a cement block step, trotting across the gravel and to Dad's passenger door.

"Welcome, Seamus," the tall man announced through a smile.

"Thank you, Tanner," Dad replied.

We each introduced or reintroduced ourselves to Dr. Tanner as we piled out of the Windstar. Dr. Tanner worked with the state's Department of Geology as a seismologist. His expertise covered the faults along Maine's coastline and activity along these fissures. Dad knew him from their time together teaching at the university, and each considered the other a close friend as well as a colleague.

Dr. Tanner once gave me a Christmas gift that baffled me. One year, when I was seven, I opened an odd shaped package that I hadn't asked for. I found a plastic drum that vibrated and twisted about. I put one of my Captain Fantastic action figures in it and watched him rattle around for a few minutes before Dad stopped the machine.

"It's a rock tumbler, Pickle," Dad told me. "You use it to polish rocks into a smooth round shape."

I thought that was an odd choice for someone who believed rocks only came in handy for skipping and throwing at the girls down the street, but I gave it a try. Twelve years later, I still used it from time to time. I couldn't remember if I liked it because of the action or the results, or if it was because the noise annoyed the hell out of Jack, but I still messed around with the thing occasionally. Since then, I'd always liked Tanner.

* * *

"Thanks for inviting me, Seamus." Tanner rested in a chair behind an oval table in the back corner of his trailer. The rest of us sat where we could find space, me against the wall on the floor, Dad in another chair beside the three-legged table, Ben cross-legged on an afghan, and Erin and Jack twisted together on a blanket near a makeshift bookcase.

"Of course, Tanner," Dad replied. "I knew you wanted to check some equipment out there, make sure it still worked."

"I really need to check to make sure they're not malfunctioning all right. If they aren't, that thing's going through some serious changes."

"What type of changes?" Erin wondered.

"I'm glad you asked, dear. You see, if the readings we're getting back at the lab are any indication, Baffert Island is an active site. In the past six months, a series of small tremors have emanated from that island, with these small quakes coming in greater numbers and with greater force in the more recent weeks. I've been meaning to get out there to make sure my equipment isn't on the blink."

"So what you're saying is ..."

"Dome of the Rock is getting ready to relieve some pressure. You see, a lava dome is nothing more than magma building pressure on the surface from beneath. The stress on the ground above slowly pushes the earth above it, creating more and more torque on the land.

"Think of it as a pimple. When the thing first appears, it grows as an enlarged bump on your face. But if you try to pop it, what happens?"

"Stuff oozes out," Jack giggled.

"Yes. The lava dome at Baffert is like that. It's pushing out like the pus in a pimple. These tiny quakes are a warning sign that the pressure has built to a point that it may be ready to pop."

"That place is gonna blow?" Erin gasped in air as the question left her lips.

"Probably not, at least not in an eruption like you might think, and most likely not while we're there. The most likely scenario involves one strong quake there, although even then a quote unquote strong quake wouldn't even probably be felt by anybody. These quakes I've described to you that are going on now are weaker than you brushing your own teeth.

"While we're there, the island will suffer probably twenty or more quakes per day. But you won't even know it unless you see the readings back at our lab."

"Phew." Erin slouched back into Jack's arms.

Tanner lit a cigarette and slid himself further into his chair. "You see, kids, you're going to get to see some cool stuff in the next couple days, stuff most people don't even know about."

"He's right," Dad added. "We're going to do some great things out there. But now we should be going. Tanner, are your things together?"

"Yes Seamus. They're all in my study."

"Let's go then."

Tanner rose from his chair, took two steps to his left, and picked up two olive duffel bags. "All set."

I shrugged my shoulders in response to my friends' quizzical looks.

Leaving last, I made sure to lock the door, although I doubted anybody would invade Tanner's private space in his absence. Even if they dared, I knew there was no way they'd find anything of value in the clutter that stretched throughout the interior of the trailer. Anything potential thieves found in Tanner's place, should they make the attempt, rightfully belonged to them based on their persistence. Nevertheless, I followed Tanner's wishes and bolted shut the door, leaving his so-called palatial estate secure.

CHAPTER 8

We pulled out of the driveway and back on the highway, heading east toward the ocean. "Where to now, Dad?" I asked, keeping my eyes on the road.

"We're going to the airfield just outside Bar Harbor." Dad lifted his glasses and rubbed under them at his eye.

"I've had it," Jack growled from the back seat. "Can't you play some better music please?"

I reached down to the floorboards and produced a compact disc. "You asked for it," I replied, sliding the disc into the player.

"Oh God no, Jared," Jack pleaded, but it was too late for him. In the recent months I had discovered something even worse than the rock tumbler to audibly assault poor Jack. I found that he had a weak spot for the party rap of the late eighties, the go-go beats and upbeat rhythms of some squeaky clean artists who just happened to produce some downright catchy tunes. I'd thrown together my own mix, burning my own compilation from selections I'd downloaded off the Internet. This compact disc, which I labeled as "Jack's Penance," provided immeasurable amusement to me, especially when Jack protested to my deaf ears.

"Sorry bro," I teased, "but you know the rule. Driver's choice."

The first track of my compilation commenced, a particularly memorable, albeit not well known, selection called "Get Up And Have A Good Time" from an artist who went by the moniker of Rob Base. The party beat and accompanying singing by some unknown vocalist sent Jack into an attempt to hide his face from the coming pain.

There was only one way to torment him further. Good thing I knew every word to the song in question. Of course, I'd trained myself by listening to the disc for weeks.

"Ah now rappers used to keep me behind the ropes,
But I didn't care because I was too dope,
Say what?
They used to down me, say I ain't,
But that's all fine cause now I'm gettin' mine,
In eighty-nine,
Drinkin' wine,
Maxin' with the girls with the nice behinds,
I used to rap with a guy named Ace,
And on his side was me, Base,
E-Z Rock in the back on the wheels,
Kurt my manager, gettin' ill,
Stickin' up kids on the block,
He met this one girl, then he stopped,
Mike and Dave was my managers then,
Let's have fun and just comprehend."

By the end of the first verse, Ben joined in with me. We both belted out the lyrics of the chorus as Jack grimaced and squirmed in his seat. I struggled not to laugh, but the fact that a song drove Jack that nuts made me smile. He deserved it, especially in response to all the hours of angry rock I'd been subjected to.

We followed the main highway toward Bar Harbor, passing through Ellsworth along the way. We used to spend a lot of time out there; in fact, we usually traveled out that far at Christmas to get a tree. There was something about that little town that always drew us back. It was more than likely the feeling that nothing could ever go bad there, that life went right in that small village. It reminded me of home. I liked every little shop, cottage, and smiling face I encountered in Ellsworth.

After we left Ellsworth, the road climbed a series of hills on its way toward the sea. The trees thinned out as we approached the airfield, a single runway off to the left of the highway. We reached the airfield around one in the afternoon, pulling up to a small building set alone along the airstrip.

Dad climbed out first and wandered to the building. He disappeared into the structure for a few minutes. We remained quiet as we waited for him, not knowing what to say to each other to pass the time.

Dad popped out of the building, followed by another gentleman who seemed to secrete grease. His upper body sported a yellowing T-shirt underneath an open lumberjack shirt, the sleeves rolled up to his elbows. His blue jeans were stained all the way down the front legs with mud, shit, something brown. His heavy feet slid across the blacktop in military style boots.

As he got closer, I noticed more about him. His face resembled a demented squirrel's, with his jutting upper teeth and receded chin, coupled with the sheer size of his hook nose. His hair, by far my favorite feature of his look, flowed back from his face, shorter in the front and sides and cascading down the back of his scalp to his shoulders.

"Jesus Christ!" Jack giggled. "Look at his mullet!"

I giggled too. This guy, for whatever reason, had kidnapped Dad and was forcing him to ask for the ransom money, as far as I could tell. I rolled down the window in Dad's presence.

"Kids," Dad said over the breeze kicking up across the plateau, "this is Joe Cheney."

"Friends call me Mullet Joe," Mullet Joe squeaked in his rodent voice.

"No shit," Jack mumbled under a snorting giggle.

"He'll be flying us by helicopter to the island," Dad explained.

"I'm the best there is," Mullet Joe added. He produced a crusty rag from his back pocket and dug a booger from his nose with it. Tanner threw open the sliding door and exited the vehicle. The rest of us remained in the van, in case we needed to make a run for it from Mr. Cheney.

"Time's wasting, kids," Dad proclaimed. "Let's load the gear and get going."

I rolled the window up from my spot in the driver's seat. "Do you believe this?" I asked the group.

"I bet he gets laid constantly," Jack quipped.

"Shush."

"Come on, he's gotta be a pimp. Look at him."

Mullet Joe ran his hands through his greasy hockey hair helmet as I shook my head and waited for Dad to finish swinging his deal with Mr. Cheney. They sealed their bargain with a handshake, and I chuckled as I watched Dad wipe his hand on his pants, trying to remove the sticky film that Mullet Joe left with him. I unlatched the driver side door and climbed out of the Windstar.

This trip was going to get interesting.

CHAPTER 9

We loaded the gear into Mullet Joe's helicopter. How this human/rodent hybrid receptacle of trash owned his own helicopter was beyond me. Anyway, we carefully transferred our equipment, essential foodstuffs, and our personal effects from the van to his helicopter while Mullet Joe inspected the craft.

Mullet Joe owned a military style helicopter, the kind used by the United States in Vietnam and subsequent wars. The official title of this aircraft was the Bell XH-40, but the common name for the helicopter was the Huey, originally named so upon its inception as a military aircraft in the mid sixties. This machine served our purpose perfectly, because much like Vietnam, we needed an aerial craft that allowed us into small spaces. We needed a vehicle that was capable of transporting six "troops" into the interior of the island itself. We required a reliable means of transportation to Baffert Island.

"This thing gonna fly?" Ben wondered aloud. "I mean, it has 'Whirlygirl' written on the side in duct tape."

Ben's observation proved correct. The word decorated the exoskeleton of the Huey, just beneath the window on the pilot's side. Whirlygirl remained the same olive drab color she no doubt wore during her military career. She even exhibited a few scars from her service time, a couple of bullet holes that punctured her skin along her sides, something similar to harpoon marks found on whales I'd seen off Bar Harbor. It became clear to me that Mullet Joe owned her as a result of her retirement, that Whirlygirl had served her time for her country and now enjoyed the quiet life, however quiet and peaceful an existence spent with Mullet Joe could possibly be.

"Oh, she'll fly," Mullet Joe replied as he patted the steel skin of his girlfriend. "I've kept her up since I bought her ten years ago. She's never let me down. Whirlygirl will do just nicely."

Mullet Joe tightened a bolt near the rear rotor with a wrench. He wiped his brow with his dirty rag and turned back toward us.

"Whirlygirl's ready."

"And she told you this?" Jack asked.

"Yes. She always tells me when she's ready."

"Great. Just checking."

I ducked into the fuselage first, glancing back at Dad as I strapped myself in. He flashed a glance over to me, diverting his attention from his discussion with Tanner. He pressed his index and middle fingers to his eyebrow, pushed them toward me, and pulled them back to his brow again. I nodded to him and offered my hand to Ben as he climbed aboard.

Once all of us were secured within her belly, Whirlygirl coughed smoke in response to Mullet Joe's gentle touch at her throttle. "It's okay girl," he gently spoke, "they won't hurt you." He turned the ignition again, and Whirlygirl stammered, her main rotor whirring to life, slowly at first but soon with great vigor. Mullet Joe gently nudged at the controls, and Whirlygirl lifted from the helipad, carefully so as not to disturb her passengers with any sort of jarring movements. As the ground grew less descriptive below us, I noticed Erin's face.

Jack had his arm draped over her left shoulder, patting her softly on her back. Her eyes peered down into the floor, and her hands were tightly clenched together in a tangled ball. Erin breathed very shallowly, gulping air in at a rapid pace, barely holding in the short gobbles of oxygen before releasing them again.

I leaned over toward her in my seat. "Are you all right?"

Jack leaned toward me. "She's afraid of heights," he bellowed over the rotor blade. "Remember how she won't ride the Parachute Drop at the fair?"

"Is she going to be okay?" I yelled back.

Erin nodded her head sheepishly in reply to my query. She refused to remove her gaze from the floor. I slid back into my seat, trying to forget how loud and bumpy our ride was.

We required the helicopter ride because of our destination. Baffert Island, the Dome of the Rock, lied off the coast among a chain of isles. Most of these islands had been created by the tectonic activity of two plates that had been grinding together since the dawn of man. At one time, some of these islands were conceivably part of the mainland but had broken away during the tectonic shift. The island was fairly remote, a tiny sibling of the islands in this chain.

Also, Baffert Island's past prevented it from being reached in a more conventional manner. When it erupted, Baffert Island littered the ocean surrounding its northern and western faces with rock. These rocks decorated the ocean floor in a jagged field, stretching out toward the mainland. Some twenty or more of these shards protruded from the ocean's surface, and many dozens of other pieces hid below the surface. The problem was nobody knew for sure how deep many of these pieces were below the surface. Dome of the Rock, although defined as a state park, really existed as a preserve. There was no ferry service to the place. The only way in was by privately chartered aircraft or by finding a way through the danger beneath the surface.

Whirlygirl followed the coastline south past Burkshire before banking softly to the east. Tree specked land gave way to pebble beaches four hundred feet below us. White foam licked the beaches as waves crashed and receded on the shores below. The churning seas below seemed no more dangerous than ripples in the bathtub from our flying fortress. The craft completed its bank, righted itself, and puttered through the air, heading almost due east.

"There she is," Mullet Joe squawked over his headset. "Baffert Island. Dome of the Rock State Park."

DOME OF THE ROCK

I inched forward to see the island through the cockpit. It seemed so small at first, mainly because we remained miles from it. But as we approached, the sheer size of what stood before us stole my breath. We lowered to about two hundred feet as we closed on the island. As we did, Mulet Joe piloted the helicopter toward the southwest corner of the island, an open area of what looked to be compacted shells or sand. In the afternoon sun, the beach glistened brightly, a creamy white color. This beach extended a good fifty to one hundred yards from tip to tip, guarded at both ends by high rock. From our perch, I noticed that the rock on the western edge of the beach seemed higher, but the rock on the southern edge appeared thicker and more complete. The western piece was a separate shard, while the southern sentinel remained connected to what remained of the mountain.

Mullet Joe banked Whirlygirl to our right, manuevering to the south. Erin groaned lightly in response to the shift of the helicopter in the sky. Whirlygirl hovered slower as we crossed over from water to land, as we entered the airspace of Baffert Island itself.

"Isn't it beautiful?" Dad called over the humming blades above us.

"Stunning," Tanner squawked back over his headset.

Whirlygirl picked up visual contact with a trail below, inside the crater and starting at the beach. Mullet Joe chose to follow the path.

"This trail leads into the core of the crater for about one and a half miles," he reported. "The parks department requests that all visitors stay on that path. Of course, since you're here under special permission, that fact will be...slackened for your purposes."

He breathed in again before continuing. "The crater is about six square miles across. The trail ends at a selected observation point under Serpent Rock at the base of the east wall. As you can see below, the trail cuts a pathway along the southern part of the crater.

"The lava dome itself is covered with vegetation, mostly Scotch broom and other such brush. The wisps of steam you see rising around us are from the dome. And...ah, here we are. Serpent Rock."

Mullet Joe slowed Whirlygirl to the point where she stood still in the sky. She stared directly at a large boulder, weighing many tons and standing at least thirty yards across and fifteen feet in height above the plateau it rested upon. The rock looked back at this electronic mosquito, with sunken spaces that resembled eyes. The monolith before us also seemed to possess an open mouth and appeared to have a coiled body that disappeared into the plateau.

A chill rose up my spine and caused the hair on my neck to stand. Something about this large boulder didn't sit well with me. It was as if the serpent and I carried a shared destiny, that somehow what I did on Baffert Island would be decided by the whim of this dormant basalt.

"It looks like a snake," Ben commented, raising his voice over the sound of the churning gears.

"That's right, son," Dad replied. "That's why it's called Serpent Rock."

"Moving on to the north wall of the crater," Mullet Joe continued, "as you can see, there's not much more than a bed of discarded fragments, extending out into the ocean and toward the horizon."

"Geologists found a piece of Baffert Island as far away as Waterville, that's how forceful the blast was." Tanner adjusted his body weight in his seat beside me as he spoke. "That rock carried itself through the air at least fifty miles, against the prevailing wind pattern, to reach that point. That's quite a power to force on an inanimate object."

"Imagine how far a dude would go," Jack laughed.

"And Jack knows what inanimate means," I joked. "Congratulations, Jack. You truly did earn that diploma." I threw my arms up to guard my face as Jack lashed out his hand at me.

DOME OF THE ROCK

Mullet Joe turned the helicopter back toward the beach at the southwest corner of the island and carefully touched her down just inside the safety of the southern wall of the crater. We waited for the rotor blades to slow, then emerged from Whirlygirl and onto solid ground.

"See anything of interest, Seamus?" Tanner inquired, scratching his chin. Us kids continued to unload the belongings as the two doctors huddled together, looking into the site.

"Nothing too important right now, Tanner," Dad replied. He rubbed his eye underneath his glasses as he spoke. "I think we'll set up camp for now, call it early tonight. Tomorrow we'll follow the trail, see what we can find with a full night's sleep and a dozen rested eyes."

Dad turned to Mullet Joe. "Mr. Cheney, you can go if you wish. I'll call you on the cell phone tomorrow, maybe arrange a closer fly-by with you if I need to."

"Sure thing, sir."

"Good day then, Mr. Cheney." Dad flashed Mullet Joe his two finger to eyebrow salute as Whirlygirl purred to life again. She lifted off the beach, kicking up dust around us as she left the constraints of gravity with us. She turned toward the north and soon slipped from view over the horizon.

"Okay kids," Dad said, "Let's set up camp. We're going to take the afternoon easy today, get to bed early tonight. Tomorrow, we find our destiny."

With that, the six of us got to work throwing up tents, building a secure fire pit, and gathering dry wood. Above us, Serpent Rock kept a watchful eye on the strangers that trespassed on its sacred plot.

CHAPTER 10

"Gather round, children. Tanner. I'd like to tell you about what we're really looking to find."

We all stepped over to the fire pit, which crackled with life as the flames kissed the slowly darkening twilight sky and the embers flipped into the air. Dad sat on a stump, which he had dragged beside the fire. Erin and Jack huddled together on the sand, while Tanner, Ben, and I shared space on a log. Dad removed his glasses, rubbed his eye, and replaced the spectacles while he cleared his throat.

"The Viking legend builds upon the same kind of idea of heaven and earth that our traditional Christian culture holds sacred, more or less. The Viking heaven is known as Asgard, the Earth Midgard. They have Hell as well. There are also other lands, places where creatures such as ice giants and dwarves come from or go to, but we're not worried about those.

"My quest comes from the Asgard and Midgard connection. When a mortal being or a god was slain on Midgard, if they died in a just and true way, a valkyrie would come and claim their soul. The valkyrie resembles an angel in some ways. This minion of the heavens would take the souls of the slain and transport them to Asgard, where they would remain for eternity in bliss.

"There was a bridge that connected Asgard to Midgard. This bridge, according to what I've come to believe, had a gate on the Midgard side which only the worthy could pass through to Asgard. The gate was guarded by two wolves, Hugin and Munin, thought and memory, which refused to allow the unworthy to pass and answered only to Odin, father of the gods. I contend that they knew the valkyries by sight, encountering these creatures frequently, and always allowed them to pass freely.

"Based on the description given by Ulric Johannsen, there are two wolves guarding what he saw during the second voyage to the End of the Earth. He claims he saw two wolves guarding a great gate at Udodelig Oy, the Island of the Immortals. Since it's known that Viking explorers reached North America, it's conceivable they got this far south. That's why we're here."

"Fascinating," I said.

Dad pointed to Serpent Rock, still watching from across the lava dome, perched high on the plateau of the east wall. "That gruesome creature is the Midgard Serpent," Dad explained. "It played a key role in the end of the world. Ragnarok.

"The end came slowly at first. The gods learned too late about the evil of one of their own, Loki, and lost the purest of gods, Balder, to his treachery. They banished Loki to Earth, where he used his cunning to corrupt the mortals. Crime ran rampant across the land.

"Sol and Mani, the sun and moon, drove their chariots in fright instead of their usual smiles. Each day they were overtaken by wolves that chased them, but they knew they were okay. However, they grew fearful and the Earth grew sad and cold. The Fimbulwinter commenced, with snow falling from all parts of the world at once, and the Earth was covered in ice.

"This winter lasted six years. During this time of severe winter, with no break, mankind became even worse. The crimes of the mortal race increased in both scope and frequency. Worst of all, the memories of compassion and caring faded from view.

"A giantess fed the three progeny of Fenris, the wolf, with the bones of the adulterers and murderers. These three wolves were so well fed that they eventually became powerful enough to catch Sol and Mani, and the world was coated with a deluge of blood when they caught their prey.

"When this happened, the entire world shook in fear. The stars fell from the sky. Loki, Fenris, and Garm, shackled in exile, all freed themselves and rushed forth to claim revenge on those who had forsaken them. At the same time, a dragon chewed through the root of the tree of life. A rooster perched above Valhalla crowed the warning, which alerted Heimdall to send out the call on his horn.

"The heroes gathered in Valhalla, mounted their horses, and rushed out to Vigrid, where the last battle was to take place. We're looking for Vigrid, because that's where the gate will be. It will be where the last battle occurred, waiting for anybody worthy enough to be accepted into the eternal afterlife."

"You sure are dropping a lot of names," Jack joked. Erin nudged him gently to get him to be quiet.

"So what happened to them?" Erin asked.

"I'm getting to that, my child. First all the fiercest foes of decency needed to assemble. The terrible Midgard Serpent, our friend on the hill top, awoke in a foul mood and thrashed about in the deep ocean. The resulting waves crashed forth throughout the world. The serpent crawled from the sea to join the battle.

"Meanwhile, the fatal ship, moored tight on land, was cast afloat by one of the waves. Loki boarded the ship and set sail for the Vigrid plain. Another ship approached from the north, loaded to the hilt with frost giants, who wanted nothing more than to put a hurting on their warm-blooded foes.

"Hel, goddess of death, emerged from her sanctuary with the Hel-hound Garm and the dragon Nidhug in tow. They reached the battlefield and were greeted warmly by Loki. They were soon joined by another merchant of evil as the sky fell and Surtr emerged. The glorious rainbow bridge collapsed as they rode across it.

"The gods themselves stood at a great disadvantage. They knew they would most likely perish in their battle, but they had to fight. Odin suffered with only one eye, a result of his quest for knowledge.

His friend Tyr would fight with only one hand, and Frey no longer possessed his invincible sword. The forces of good marched to the battlefield, while Odin rode to the fountain of knowledge, where he found the tree of life toppling over. He conferred with Mimir one last time then returned to his waiting forces.

"The two forces gathered, sizing each other up. Finally, in an instant of overflowing hatred, the battle was joined. Odin and the Fenris wolf matched up, mighty Thor attacked the Midgard Serpent, and Tyr faced off with Garm. Frey met Surtr, and Heimdall engaged Loki, and the other combatants squared off in a terrible series of battles.

"The father of the gods was among the first to die. Odin struggled with the Fenris wolf, which grew larger by the moment as the evil inside it welled up. Finally, it stretched its jaws from Heaven to Earth, and it rushed forth with its open mouth and swallowed Odin whole.

"Nobody had a chance to save Odin. Frey tried to fight back against Surtr, but he soon was run through by Surtr's flaming sword. Heimdall fell next, losing a tough struggle with Loki. Garm took care of Tyr in a similar tragic fashion. That left Thor and the Midgard Serpent.

"Thor used his hammer to finish off the snake with one forceful shot to its skull. Exhausted, Thor staggered for nine steps. At that point, the poisonous venom stored within the snake flowed across the land. Thor drowned in the deluge that escaped the now dead snake.

"By the way, I don't think that up there is a rock. It's my belief that it's a fossil."

I pushed myself to the ground from my seated position on the log. Resting my back against the wood, I listened as Dad continued.

"Another hero, Vidar, appeared at the scene, although it was now far too late. The forces of good lay dead all across the battlefield. However, Vidar had been prophesied as the one who would take down the Fenris wolf, and he rushed forth to engage the beast. He held the lower jaw fast with his foot, and grabbed the upper jaw and killed the wolf with a gruesome twist."

Jack grunted, "Cool."

"Surtr claimed the Earth with his fiery brands. A great fire ensued, which burned everything until the blackened land fell beneath the boiling waters of the sea. At that point, the Earth, for all intents and purposes, was dead."

"Is that it?" Erin asked. She held her chin up with her right hand, right elbow rested on her right knee.

"In some cases that's where it ends. However, the story I tend to believe tells us that the Earth rose from its watery grave. A new charioteer drove what Sol once piloted, guiding the sun on its journey across the sky. Two mortals had survived when they hid in the forest and had slept through the destruction. They started life anew and greater than before.

"The heavens also recovered. Descendants of the now deceased gods came forth and searched for a sign of survival. It took them awhile, but they discovered that the highest heavenly fortress had been above the destruction. This highest heavenly place became the home for the truly virtuous."

Dad relaxed his shoulders upon completion of his story. He breathed in deeply once, twice, and poked a stick into the fire, rustling the embers. He scratched his forehead then spoke once more.

"The reason we're here is simple. In every piece of folklore one can find at least a shred of fact. For example, the idea of Sol and Mani comes from the path of the sun and moon across the sky. Ulric Johannsen saw something that he wrote down in irrefutable terms. There's a rock that is a serpent's head on top of a steep cliff, a cliff which wouldn't exist if the mountain didn't blow itself apart a thousand years ago. We're going to find it here. We will find the site of Ragnarok."

"Seamus," Tanner countered, "you're enthusiasm is no doubt infectious. However, I find it hard at best to believe in what you're saying. I mean no disrespect, but the likelihood of a gate to the heavens existing is suspect. Plus, there's the matter of how something like that ended up falling, intact, into an exposed crater."

"That's why I confide in you, Tanner. You always provide the tough questions that serve only to prove my ideas as sound. Allow me a demonstration. If it works, we stay for the two days, try to find Ragnarok. If I fail, I'll call Mr. Cheney tonight and arrange for us to leave tomorrow morning. Fair?"

"Sure."

Dad stood in the advancing twilight and walked a few steps toward the water's edge. "I'm going to build a mound right here," he explained, stooping over and taking a seat in the sand. We all followed him and gathered around. Dad dug in the fine powdery sand, scooping the dust into a small mound. He put his right hand into the dirt and continued to build his mound, burying his own hand with his remaining free left hand.

"Okay. This mound represents the plot of land we currently inhabit before it blew. Could someone wet this down please?"

Ben and I rushed to the sea's edge. We scooped up handfuls of water and ran back to Dad and his sculpture, throwing our liquid loads on his creation.

"This will represent the gate to Asgard," Dad continued. He fished into his pocket with his free left hand. He pulled a small green object from within his pocket and set it down beside him.

"Is that ..." Erin started.

"Yes," Dad replied, cutting her off. "It's a Monopoly house. It'll serve my purpose just fine."

Dad smoothed out the top of his mound. "Johannsen wrote that the top of this island mountain was flat. Remnants of that fact are under Serpent Rock. The final battle took place on a plain near the sea. I'll assume no one has a problem believing that this mound should be flat on top."

We all nodded in agreement that Dad's assumption was fair. Dad grasped the Monopoly piece and placed it on the flat plateau. "If my theory is correct, when I recreate the eruption, this house will ride the back of the top of this mound into the exposed crater. It will land in the basin remaining, face up and in perfect shape. If not, we'll pack up tomorrow."

We all fell silent as Dad prepared. He took in one more breath, thought for a second, and rapidly pushed his right hand from the mound, forcing the dirt in a similar direction to where the rock littered the ocean from the eruption. We stayed silent for a moment, looking down at the lonely green plastic house, lying in the exposed hole left by Dad's now removed hand.

Finally, Tanner spoke up. "Well, we have a big day ahead of us tomorrow." He turned and headed back toward camp.

"Cool, Dad," I added, stooping over and picking up the Monopoly piece, which rested flat inside the model crater. I handed it to Dad before looking up to the east. As the sun slipped from view behind us, the last shine of the orb flickered off the serpent's face. The serpent did not look pleased.

CHAPTER 11

Everyone decided to follow Dad's advice and enter into slumber early that evening. We all crashed in sleeping bags, two people per tent. Jack protested when his request to sleep with Erin received a denial. Erin shared a tent with Dad, Ben with Jack, and me with Tanner. A dark sky hung over us that evening, filled only with thousands upon thousands of faintly twinkling stars.

It was a well known fact that people who lived in trailers snored loud enough to awaken the long since dead. It stemmed from the rampant weight problems that many trailer people suffered from, but that never fully explained the phenomenon. Besides, Tanner lacked the girth of somebody who normally suffered this nighttime affliction. Whatever the case may be, Tanner's vocal night sleeping caused me to vacate the tent in the middle of the night.

I wandered down to the shore and watched the dark water for a bit. The peaceful repetition of the spooky churning sea brought a calm over my body. I felt at home against that backdrop, and the thought of the serene beauty of that scene, a natural spot left untouched by human progress, filled my soul with a sense of ease. I sat, then laid, in the sand, shifting my gaze to the stars above. Each twinkling light continued to soothe my sleepless body, bringing an overwhelming feeling of inner joy to me. I could see myself spending every day in a setting like this, and it made me happy to live in such a place as Maine.

I stayed on the beach, alone for probably forty-five minutes, before my peaceful feeling found itself interrupted. I'd been in an almost hypnotic state when I felt a presence watching me. I blinked awake as a shadow fell on me, a shadow created as a result of the still rising moon. I rose from my back to a seated position and turned to greet whoever or whatever had decided to join me.

"Hi," Erin whispered on the night breeze. The moon illuminated the best parts of her: her cornsilk hair, her shapely frame, her perfect dimensions. She carried a wool blanket with her, pulled tightly about her shoulders, over the top of a long sleeve shirt and flannel sweat pants.

"Hey," I replied, also in a hushed voice. My attire, in comparison, was irrelevant. I wore some sloppy combination of sweats and long sleeves, my Caesar haircut more like a Caesar salad of a hairdo after spending three hours tossing around on an inflatable pillow.

"Mind if I join you?" Erin asked. "Jack won't leave me be. He keeps tapping on the wall of the tent with his penis."

"No problem," I replied.

Erin planted herself close beside me, to my left. She immersed herself in the dark churning before us.

"Sometimes I wish he would just stop," she began. "It's always about kiss this and sex that. He's spent the past couple hours trying, but I'm just not interested. Not here anyway. Not with your dad sleeping in the same tent as me. Definitely not where all of you can hear us."

"Not a problem to me," I retorted. "I wouldn't want to do him either."

Erin stifled a laugh, stuffing her mouth under the wool blanket.

"Listen," I said, "I've never understood why Jack got so lucky."

"So lucky?" Erin replied.

"So lucky," I repeated. "You know, he gets to have the best of you. I've known you my whole life, and in the time you've known me, how lucky have I been? Let's see, there was the psycho in ninth grade Stephanie. Then there was what I call the lost years. Now it seems the only woman I can attract is someone like Mattressback, nothing but sluts. Most guys wouldn't complain."

"But you're not most guys. In fact, I've never met another man like you."

I looked her in her eyes for the first time that night. Something in them told me that she wanted something better, something more than what she was getting from Jack. The gaze coming back at me displayed nothing but sorrow in the situation.

"Is everything all right?" I asked.

"Well…pretty much. I'm just not sure. I mean…why can't Jack be…more like…well, more like you?"

"He tries. He's just not good at expressing himself, that's all. Like, when he walked from graduation, I know he stewed the whole way home, but he never talked to anyone about what happened."

"I know. But that's not right. He should talk to me about those things. I always listen. I just don't think he likes me like that." Erin's eyes started to glisten with moisture in the moonlight.

I reached my left arm around her and pulled her closer. "Don't cry," I whispered into her ear. "It's going to be okay. I promise."

"I just wish he was more like you."

"I wish I was him."

At that point, I wished that words could magically return to your lips. That sentence, no matter how true, shouldn't have slipped from my mind and into the real world.

"What?"

I couldn't turn back from where I'd taken the talk. "I wish…that I was the one, the one with you."

"What?"

"It's always been you, Erin. Always." With that, I leaned over and closed my eyes.

That kiss we shared told her everything I wanted to. I kissed her to thank her for all the times we supported each other, through the tough times, the breakups, chicken pox, skinned knees, broken bones, and the flu. That kiss apologized for all the fights, failed relationships with others, for not allowing her to help build forts, and for smacking her with sticks. It reminded her of the trips to baseball games, road trips down the coast, summer camps, and band practices. The kiss promised her everything she ever wanted in life, from a man, a companion, and a friend. And it served to let her know that, no matter what, she'd never find herself hurt again. I wouldn't allow it.

All that came from a shared kiss that lasted only seconds but was a lifetime in the making. As I pulled away and opened my eyes, I noticed that she still held fast, in the pale moonlight, yearning to be loved like that forever. The first kiss with someone you love more than life itself can only be matched by each successive shared moment with that special person. That kiss is special, to be sure, and will never be surpassed, but it's not meant to be. Each and every moment with someone you care for will forever remain just as important, and that's what I thought of as Erin thanked me for the talk, stood, and wandered back to camp. I remained bathed in the pale night air, melting into the calming voice of the sea and the gentle embrace of Baffert Island itself.

At least my secret was out. Now, just maybe, what I wanted would come to me. For once.

CHAPTER 12

I couldn't remember the last time I awoke with the dawn. More than likely, the last time I'd done that came from some fishing trip or another appointment that required me to rise with the sun itself. In my younger years, waking before there were four digits on my alarm clock when unnecessary never happened.

However, the new day dawned and erected a beam of light into the vinyl tent walls. The shine of the sunlight through the surface caused the tent to glow orange and served as my unofficial wake up call. I rolled in my bag for a few moments, exited the tent, and proceeded to urinate away the morning drowsiness I carried with me to the thicket of brush.

"Morning, Jared," Ben grumbled gruffly. Like me, his peaceful slumber had dissipated along with the shadows of night.

"Morning, Dewey," I replied under my breath.

"Good day for a hike," he coughed through a rough throat. The clear air of the island, even compared with the relatively pollution free environment we came from, still needed getting accustomed to.

Over the next half an hour, the remainder of our bunch emerged from their sleeping quarters one by one. Dad, Tanner, Erin, and Jack each poked their heads from their tents in turn and greeted the day in their separate fashions. Perhaps Jack said it best when he growled defiantly at the sun, telling the gaseous orb to go to hell. I laughed, mostly at him because I always found it funny when something bothered my brother.

"Jack," Dad muttered, "bring us the breakfast rations."

Jack rummaged in his backpack, digging deep into the main compartment, before he produced a paper sack. He unrolled the folded opening of the bag and reached inside. In turn around the circle, Jack handed each of us a small packet, an individual meal in a clear cellophane package. We all looked at what rested in our hands for a moment, speechless, before Dad finally broke the silence of our awe.

"Son, these are Twinkies."

"Yes, they sure are, Dad."

Dad thought carefully before continuing. "Son, I asked you to buy breakfast rations."

"I did. Just like you said."

Dad breathed in deeply before continuing once again. "How?"

The one word sentences had started.

"You said get something that wouldn't take much to prepare. Something easy and quick. Something non-perishable."

"Son."

"Twinkies can survive Armageddon, Dad. They're indestructible."

"Sure."

Dad looked down at the snack cake in his left hand. He scratched his widow's peak with his right hand, thinking of what to say next.

"Fine."

The discussion ended there. We all knew it. Each of us slowly unwrapped our Twinkies and snacked on them. Jack's face seethed with anger, an obvious slap to his ego having been provided by his own stepfather. He finished first, forcefully destroying his confection with his teeth.

* * *

"How long do you think checking your instruments will take, Tanner?"

"Not long, Seamus. It's all just the matter of reaching them and making a quick field check."

"It's eight-thirty now. We should head out soon. We'll take it slow on the trail, make sure we don't miss anything important."

Dad turned, looking from Tanner to his left. We all walked up beside him. Looking up toward the direction of the still climbing sun, our eyes settled on the figure before us. The target of our combined awakening stares sized us up in kind, almost daring us to enter its lair. Serpent Rock awaited our assault on its home.

CHAPTER 13

We left most of our equipment at camp as we left the beach area. Since our base was hidden behind the shelter of the western point of the island, a sheer wall of rock, we felt confident that no pirates would come and snatch our precious tents and personal effects. We each slapped a pack onto our backs and began to climb the trail leading into the Dome of the Rock.

Tanner took the point position, followed closely by Dad. Jack and Erin followed in tandem, then Ben and me in a final row of two. The trail briefly followed the interior of the southwestern cliff, but within a tenth of a mile veered sharply toward the north. The trail cut a swath across an incline within the crater, a tactic used to make the climb less hazardous to both environment and hiker. We crested the hill, finding the area flat as we reached an even sharper bend in the trail. We'd walked about a quarter mile in just under half an hour.

"Stunning," Dad proclaimed as he crested the small incline and reached the pronounced bend. He and Tanner both stopped at this spot and breathed in the surroundings.

The scene before us reminded me of the meadow on the Carter farm back home. Looking out, I saw nothing but lush vegetation as far as possible across the crater floor. The underbrush and tall grasses stood no more than three feet high clear across the crater, extending nearly to the far edge of the interior. The brush grew sparser near the huge boulders and outcroppings that littered the northern regions of the island's interior, but life still flourished there as well. It resembled a blanket covering the floor of the island's interior, with the less overgrown areas looking like wrinkles in the blanket, as if it hadn't been laid flat. Some flowers showed signs of blooming, and a gentle breeze created waves in this sea of vegetation.

Tanner patted Dad on his shoulder with his left hand. "Your dream lies somewhere out there," he said. Adjusting his pack on his shoulders, he turned to us. "Come on, kids. Our first stop is not far."

The trail twisted sharply to the northeast from where we stood. It straightened out in front of us, and I noticed that the trail climbed sharply ahead. Whoever planned this path chose to be as unobtrusive as possible. They wanted the site preserved as much as could be, keeping visitors off the bulk of the island. Their choice of path took us up a steep incline, hugging close to the southern wall.

"This sucks," Jack complained as we slowly struggled up the face of the trail. Loose dirt slipped under our feet. Traction eluded our boots. We took turns stopping and hydrating ourselves as we climbed this steep and seemingly endless incline. It leveled off for a few yards and then rose again. Just when I thought I could take no more, Tanner dropped his pack from his shoulders and stepped to the left of the trail, toward the north.

He bent over and squatted low along the edge of the trail. Pulling a screwdriver from his pocket, he pushed dusty gravel from an object that extended a few inches above the ground. It glimmered in the sun as Tanner scooped away dirt from around it. He stabbed at it with his screwdriver, twisting at it with the tool until its cylindrical top popped from it. He placed the top next to it and peered inside.

"Everything looks good," he remarked. We inched closer around him to get a better look at the contraption buried in the ground.

Inside this machine, a needle followed a path along a circular spool. This needle ground along endlessly, leaving a track on the cylinder's surface. Looking at the spool, I could see that there wasn't a perfect line. Instead, the needle occasionally would jump, producing a jagged line, a series of sharp angles up and down on the surface. All this happened inside a small box, buried within the earth, exposed to us through a cylindrical opening in its top.

"Each series of sharp lines you see is a separate earthquake," Tanner explained. "They look impressive, but like I said, you can't even feel most of them. For example, this line here occurred last night about ten-thirty. Bet you didn't feel that, but you were at or near the epicenter." He pointed at a series of sharp waves on the meter's surface.

"This is just a field seismograph. We have larger versions of this same machine at the Department of Geology. This one mostly measures activity here at the island. Ours back at the lab can detect tremors, depending on the magnitude, from thousands of miles away. This one might pick up a truly catastrophic earthquake from elsewhere, but mostly it'll just measure what goes on here.

"Seamus, this one's working just fine."

Tanner replaced the lid and screwed it tight. He once more buried it with dirt, leaving just enough exposed to find it with the naked eye the next time he needed to check it.

As Tanner completed his task, Dad fished out binoculars from his backpack. He carefully scanned the area below us on the crater floor, looking for any clue to the whereabouts of Ragnarok. "Not here," he lamented as he pushed the binoculars back into his pack.

I began to think about my life in the past as the trail leveled off before us. My mind drifted from thought to thought, keeping alive memories of different events that happened when I was younger. As the trail continued to hug the interior southern wall, I continued to reflect on how I got to this point, how I ended up where I was. One story in particular jumped into my head as I followed the path.

Shortly after I turned nine, my little league team went to Portland for a tournament. We all played on the team: Jack, Ben, even Erin. Jack played shortstop, Ben right field just like Dwight Evans, and

Erin left field, while I pitched or played second base. Our team was competitive, not great, but we never got embarrassed by anybody throughout the year. The tournament we ventured to determined what team would represent our region in the sectional qualifying tournament later that summer.

We didn't do much at that tourney, probably lost two quick games and went home. My memory of that trip didn't come from the play on the field itself. It was what happened during the off time that I never forgot.

After our first game, a few of us walked over from the baseball complex to a corner grocery mart. Jack, Jeff Mackey, and I all wandered over there for some candy. We strutted in there like we owned the place, which quickly caught the attention of the owner, a bowling ball with a head that sat behind the counter, watching any movement in the place.

"Bet you he won't notice," Jack dared me as he handed me the Mr. Goodbar. My hands trembled and grew greasy with sweat as I kept my eyes glued to Brunswick Man behind the counter. He had a steady eye on the three of us, mainly because Jeff couldn't seem to stop fidgeting with his jock strap in the candy aisle.

"Come on, Jared," Jeff goaded, "he won't know." Jeff scratched himself as he looked over the selection of fruit favored snacks.

"I don't know ..." I protested, rather meekly. I wanted to take the candy bar, show these two losers what I had in me. Only problem was, I didn't want to be caught. I continued to shake as I watched the attendant.

"Help you find anything?" he called out from behind the counter.

"No sir," I replied, an uneven tremble in my throat.

Brunswick Man stooped over in his chair, ducking for a moment behind the counter. As he did so, I hastily shoved the Mr. Goodbar up and under my shirt, then tucked the garment within my belt. His head popped up again as I patted down my jersey. He scowled and

turned toward us as we stepped up to his cash register.
Jack and Jeff paid for their fists of goodies and we walked out of the store. We got outside the doors and they started snacking on their candy. I pulled the chocolate bar from under my shirt and tore the wrapper. As I did so, I felt a cold piece of metal press against my temple.

"I knew you'd steal from me," Brunswick Man growled. His meaty right hand extending toward me, engulfing in its grip a steel object. His index finger poked through a hole in the device and wrapped around a small protrusion within the hole. He kept the object trained on the side of my head as he continued.

"You kids think you're so great, don't you? Don't you! Well, how're you gonna feel with your brains splattered all over the pavement? Huh?!?"

I fell to my knees when I realized this guy wanted to shoot me. He continued to hold the pistol to my head as I started sobbing on the ground. I held the candy bar away from me, hoping he'd take it back.

"Please mister," I bawled, "please don't shoot me. I didn't mean to."

"You didn't mean to?" he growled. "What the fuck do you mean you didn't mean to? You stuffed it in your shirt! It didn't fall there!"

"I know," I cried. "I'm sorry. I'm sorry! I'm sorry!"

I repeated those words over and over, each time getting more hysterical. The guy refused to take the gun from my head.

"I have every right to shoot you," he roared. "I'm allowed to defend myself against thieves. I've killed men before."

"Please sir no," I begged. Tears rolled down my face, dampening the front of me.

His finger tensed around the trigger.

I dropped the candy bar and felt a warm sticky sensation in my pants. A puddle began to form around me on the concrete. I looked down at myself, at my wetted pants, and whimpered deeper.

Brunswick Man backed away at the sight of the urine puddle trickling beneath me. "Jesus Christ! You little bitch!" He removed his finger from contact with the trigger and waddled back into his corner store.

Jack and Jeff helped me from the ground, and I cried the rest of the day, renewing my tears with each laugh and point from another of the seemingly inexhaustible supply of strangers who happened upon me at the field. Coach was kind enough to find me a change of clothes eventually, but by then the damage had been done. I never again stole from another man. Jack shoplifted often, but I had no right to frown upon him after my misadventure, so I chose to ignore rather than scold.

As I continued to guard our band from a rear assault, I smiled. Remembering such a horrible event in a fond way kept me sane. I knew I was better for the experience, and no matter what occurred in life, nobody could take that away from me. As the six of us continued our quest for the gate to Asgard, following the path along the southern interior border, I chuckled softly, knowing that I'd soon have another fond memory to add to my already charmed life.

CHAPTER 14

As we plodded on into the afternoon, the monotony of the walk, the weight of our knapsacks on our backs, and the rough terrain all combined to cut into our collective enthusiasm. Once the trail leveled out, it followed a ridge tucked under the safety of the southern facade. The cliff to our right, the barrier between us and the ocean, rose high into the air. Its jagged summit cut up and down, reminding me of the insignificant squiggles Tanner insisted on checking out inside his precious machinery. He required the data they recorded for whatever stupid reason he alone cared about, and far be it for one of us to think otherwise. My mindset changed from that of fun thoughts to that of bitter tidings for all scientists as my legs screamed at me in agony, my feet crying for freedom from their separate cramped prisons of boots. My shoulders burned to the bone, losing their fight with the unforgiving straps of my backpack. It was hard to say whether or not I lost consciousness at any point, but since some of the details of the hour or so of our version of the Bataan Death March evaded my memory, I assumed that I at least entered some sort of altered state. I probably saw the mountain on fire under the unimpeded rays of the scorching sunlight. The vast thicket of underbrush below us within the crater probably taunted me. I spotted a flock of gulls overhead and expected them to dive in to rip apart my carcass once I finally collapsed.

I locked in on Serpent Rock as the trail began to dip and move to our left. The sinister visage of the snake stared down at me. A chill entered my back and found its way from my neck down my spine to my tailbone. That rock, impossible as it seemed, always kept a watch on us. No matter where we moved, Serpent Rock had its sunken crevices of eyes fixed on our progress. *I will beat you*, I thought to myself as my feet wearily dragged my body along the pathway. *No you won't*, the wind whispered back, at least in my head.

Tanner and Dad showed little ill effect of the predicament befalling us younger folk. They seemed impervious to the perils of the relentless sun, the foreboding terrain, and the sheer insanity of the pace we kept. They chatted constantly, discussing topics that only a small sliver of the minority in the world would even attempt to surmise. They talked shop, an area that only they occupied, while the four of us struggled to maintain our upright status. Tanner inspected his second unit in a space where the trail dropped into the mouth of a gully. The ground was muddy in the area, but unfortunately no water could be found to splash one another with.

Of the four of us, Ben showed the least amount of wear and tear. His background in mountaineering gave him proper preparation for our task at hand. He relished the daunting challenge in front of us, increasing the pace of his steps during the most difficult stretches. Ben hung close to Dad and Tanner while the rest of us lagged behind.

"I knew I picked the wrong week to go off my diet," Jack joked, breathless, as he stumbled and nearly fell off the trail. His tongue fought with all its might to create those few words and push them out into a sentence. He swayed slightly before catching his balance and continuing on.

Erin worried me the most. Despite her healthy exterior, she struggled the most with the hike. I began to stay with her, stopping to make sure she didn't fall too far behind the rest. She constantly swabbed sweat from her hairline, wiping at her brow with the back of her bare arms. Areas of moisture stained the front of her forest green tank top in a cross pattern across her chest. She seemed to continually adjust her pack with shoulder shrugs and strap tugs, never fully achieving an acceptable level of comfort with the process. I wanted to take her load for her, and I would have if I wasn't already dying in the act of carrying my own bag.

"Take a break, children," Dad yelled back at us from his spot further up the trail. We stumbled forward to his position before dropping our bags from our shoulders to the dirt. I let my body fall to Earth in a heap, crumpling in a pile on the edge of the trail. Jack and Erin followed my lead, collapsing to the ground under the exhaustion. We claimed separate victories over the lids of our canteens and drowned ourselves in fresh water.

"Take it slow," Ben warned us. "Too much too fast and you'll cramp up."

"Cramp on this," Jack replied, flashing his middle finger at Ben. He let his head flop lifelessly onto his backpack.

"I'm serious," Ben said.

"Me too," Jack retorted.

"Would the twin jackbastards please shut up," I muttered, generating all the energy I could muster to speak.

Tanner squatted off the trail, checking his third instrument. Dad left his side and joined our group. He wore a sweatband around his head, the black one he usually used during his wars on the handball court. Despite Dad's mounting number of handicaps, he seemed better off than all of us, the young ones who should've been able to run circles around his old ass.

"You kids all right? Pickle?"

"Yeah Dad," I muttered, "We'll make it. It's the up and down, up and down that's killing us."

"I know. Listen, go ahead and leave your packs here. We'll pick them up on the way back."

"Thanks."

"We'll move on in five minutes." Dad rubbed his eye under his glasses as he slowly walked back up trail to Tanner's side.

"I'll be dead in four," Jack replied. I attempted to take a swing at him but my exhausted limb fell well short.

The four of us rose to our feet. We resembled a platoon of soldiers in Vietnam, at least the Hollywood version. I wore a white short sleeved T-shirt, stained with both dirt and sweat. My legs were covered in olive colored cargo pants, with my canteen shoved into the large outer pocket on my left leg. The pants sagged slightly under the weight of my water bottle. I dabbed at my brow with my exposed forearms and licked salty sweat from my lips.

Ben wore a Red Sox T-shirt and a pair of denim shorts which extended to just above his knees. He kept his flask in a belt holster on his left hip. He bore a red handkerchief over his scalp, tied in a knot in the back.

Jack was stripped to the waist and wore blue jeans. He tied his white long sleeved shirt around his waist. Despite his habits and lack of exercise, Jack somehow maintained a muscular built frame. His waist tapered down beneath his pectorals. A six-pack almost protruded from his tight abdominal region. He displayed a physical build, obviously through sheer luck. His Red Sox cap, pulled tight over his eyes and rimmed with a wet ring, adorned his head.

Erin adjusted the green tank she wore by tying the lower edge in a knot. Her exposed midriff glistened in the sun, a flat stomach, not cut but better, soft and feminine. She still showed a little of her sprinter muscle. She wore a pair of khaki shorts, tan and coated with dust on the fronts of her legs. Her tan boots completed her hiking gear, that and a small scrape on her left knee.

"God!" Jack exclaimed. "You know how I like it when you're all sweaty!"

"Come on Jack," she replied.

"Listen, we could duck off for a few minutes. There's lots of bushes here. Don't you find it romantic?"

I looked at Erin as the words left Jack's mouth. She caught my glance and quickly cast her eyes away. Her mouth frowned and she took a step away from me.

"It's nice," she softly remarked.

"So come on," Jack pleaded.

"We can't," she replied. "I'm riding the Radio Flyer."

Jack stepped back from Erin.

"I know how you don't like that," she said as she strode away from us and up the trail toward Dad and Tanner. Jack waited a moment before following her.

Ben stood next to me with a perplexed look on his face.

"What is it, Ben?"

"What did she mean, riding the Radio Flyer?"

"Oh. That. She's on her red wagon, that's all."

"Gotcha."

Ben and I joined the group, and the six of us continued on.

CHAPTER 15

The walk went faster without all the cumbersome gear. It helped that the ground was more solid, the footing more sure, and the terrain less cruel. We covered the final half mile of territory in little more than a half hour.

We reached a circular point on top of a ridge at the trail's end. This flat area sat on top of a high mound. The ground sloped softly downhill from this spot in all directions, even as it reached the sharp face of the southeastern wall. The field of grass and Scotch broom stretched out below.

Jack wrapped his arms around Erin from behind her and planted his lips lightly against her neck. "Thanks," he whispered to her as they shared the view before them, the entire floor of the lava dome. In the distance, across the island, boulders rose from the floor, averaging a height of fifteen feet and a girth of ten to twenty feet around. These jagged outposts littered the landscape. Further into the distance, more outcroppings pockmarked the ocean, and white foam built up as waves crashed against them.

Dad continued to scan the island with his binoculars. He'd done this at different spots along the trail, choosing areas where we reached our highest points to take a peek at the area around us. Each attempt to find a clue to the desired location of the gate was met with a view of tall grass, faint steam, and the occasional gull or sandpiper darting into and out of the scene. With each passing wrong turn, I noticed the demeanor of Dad continue to change. His breathing provided the first clue, as it grew more audible and more forced before each continuation of the hike. His furrowed brow added to the signs, and the capper came with the first kick of dirt that Dad threw. Dad rarely, if ever, cursed out loud, but the profanity flowed out of his actions more frequently than in a Chris Rock rant.

Dad scanned the countryside slowly, passing over several spots on the horizon more than once each. He squinted through the eyepiece, running commentary to Tanner as he looked the island over. "It got to be here somewhere," he spoke through pursed lips.

Tanner completed his final field check on his equipment, finding the fourth and final seismograph in the same condition as the others. Brushing his hands on his pants, he sauntered up beside Dad.

"What now, Seamus?"

"The only thing I can think of is to get a better look."

"How so?"

"I know it must be hidden in the brush somewhere. I haven't caught a glimpse of any gleaming yet or any other sign of the site. It's unfortunate too. I couldn't ask for a better day."

"You taking the helicopter up then?"

Dad put down the binoculars. "I have little choice." He pulled the cell phone from his hip pocket and quickly dialed a number.

After a quick talk on the phone, he hung up and turned to us. We waited patiently, scattered about on the observation point. My line of sight remained transfixed on the rock littered area at the northwestern corner of the island. The sheer force it took to throw that many tons of rock into the sea boggled my mind. After all, where we stood, according to Dad, once rested over a hundred feet above us, on top of what was a mountain in the sea. Now we stood a precious few yards above the water, inside an active volcano.

"Let's go, kids. We're going back to camp. You can rest and get cleaned up while I get a detailed aerial view of the island."

As we left, I looked over my shoulder. Serpent Rock still watched us, not moving, staring at us from its perch atop the precipice. I flipped my middle finger at the inanimate object and cursed it under my breath.

* * *

The walk back to camp proved uneventful. Because of our weary natures, we remained in quiet contemplation, preferring the company of our own thoughts. I kept my eyes on the ground before me, rarely lifting them from there. We marched single file down the trail, barely stopping to gather our packs before moving on. The hike back seemed to move much quicker, almost like the long struggle in liberated us of any further punishment. Either that or we'd gone numb and no longer existed on this plane of being.

Upon reaching base camp, I dropped to my knees and forced my shoes off my feet. My poor toes throbbed with pain. I swore I heard my big toe start crying when I slipped off my socks. I crawled for a few feet before I pulled myself upright and I joined the line that staggered to the water's edge.

I didn't understand how the early settlers did it. Maybe they never bathed, or perhaps they just ventured inland, ducking Indians until they found a freshwater spring or lake. Whatever the case, keeping clean must have been a chore. Every one of us except Dad waded into the surf to get clean of our collective salty odor. However, saltwater doesn't lend a hand in the department of cleanliness. No matter how hard we scrubbed, we couldn't avoid feeling at least a little dirty. My hair remained matted to my head, and my armpits felt grainy.

We splashed about, passing a bar of soap around from person to person. The men stripped to their underpants while Erin undressed to a red bra and checkered boxers. She and I continued our earlier game of keep away with our eye contact. I'd look at her and she'd quickly avert her eyes then glance at me when she thought

I was turned. Jack and Ben wrestled each other in waist high water, and Tanner stood off to the side by himself. After a few minutes of frolicking in the shriveling surf, we returned to land and took turns changing clothes in our respective tents. I slumped to the ground outside my tent, choosing to let the sand support my weight instead of my exhausted legs. I laid my head back and allowed my body to go limp. As I begun to nod off, I could hear the approaching hum and sputter of rotor blades. I opened my eyes for a brief moment, saw that it was Whirlygirl and not a winged angel coming to carry me off, and I let my eyelids flutter shut again.

CHAPTER 16

"Children, gather around please." Dad's words dragged me from my unconscious state, curled up in the sand with a piece of driftwood tucked under one arm. I slowly stirred and rolled toward my stomach.

"What's up, Dad?" I asked as I struggled to my feet. Brushing off my legs, I noticed the others slowly returning from wherever each had disappeared to. Jack was the last to appear, emerging from his tent after everyone else had gathered around Dad.

"I found one more option to check out here on the island." Dad carried a small notepad with him, which he looked over as he spoke to us. "Tomorrow we're going to explore a small cavern I spotted under Serpent Rock. It seems likely to me that what we're looking for may be hidden in that cave."

I scratched my scalp. "I thought you said that the gate fell into the crater, like your demonstration on the beach."

"That was the most likely scenario I could envision, Pickle. However, after careful study of the area, it seems unlikely that it's out there. I can't find any trace of the Ragnarok site in the basin."

"So how could it be in a cave?" Jack questioned. He sipped from a flask. The stench of liquor wafted through the air.

"Remember when we went to New Mexico a couple years ago?" Dad replied. "When we explored that Pueblo city carved into the side of the cliffs?"

That trip to New Mexico was fun to say the least. We hiked out into the desert outside of Roswell and came across a great city that had been built into the side of the bluff. Our guides told us about how the tribe lived there for decades, uninterrupted until the westward expansion of the white man in the nineteenth century. The adobe huts and intricate pathways in this cliff protected the colony from rival groups, based on its remote location and limited access to outsiders. A picture of the cliff city was on the wall at home, in a frame in the front hallway.

"Like I've said before, many of these mythical places and relics have basis in fact. Maybe what Ulric Johannsen saw was a front used to protect the true gate to Asgard. It's a similar concept to the Holy Grail, where the true chalice, believed by many of my colleagues, is not a jewel encrusted golden drinking cup but rather a plain cup used by a common man, a carpenter. The chalice pictured in paintings is probably a decoy, and like in legend, he who chooses the correct version will attain its power. Choosing a grand goblet over a plain cup can be a fatal mistake.

"Maybe the key to the secret of Ragnarok isn't an ornate gate but rather the simple entrance of a cave in the side of a mountain. It's the same kind of concept as the tombs of the pharaohs in Egypt."

Tanner spit a cherry pit into the dirt. "You mean there's a cave up there? I've never heard of that existing."

"Sure," Dad explained, "It's right up there." He pointed toward Serpent Rock. "If you look closely, it's just below and to the left of the rock."

Tanner squinted. "I don't see where you mean."

"Trust me. It's there. I wouldn't have seen it either except for the fact that the setting sun illuminated it from the west.

"I know it's a long shot, but tomorrow is the summer solstice. Maybe the gate is like Stonehenge, where it lines up with the sun on the longest day of the year. It's iffy at best, Tanner, but at this point it's worth checking."

Tanner shrugged his shoulders. "Okay," he reluctantly agreed, "I guess we have little option." He thought for a moment. "If you say it's a burrow into the wall, then how will we reach it?"

"Simple. We take the helicopter to the plateau above then climb down. There's a ledge above the cave entrance we can reach."

Ben perked up. "You mean we're going to repel in?"

"If that's what you call it, yes. You brought the equipment I requested?" Dad lifted his glasses and rubbed his eye.

"Yes sir!"

Dad looked over the circle. "If any of you doesn't wish to take part, let me know. I won't force you into anything."

Each of us looked around the circle until eventually all of our eyes fell on Erin. She breathed in slowly and stared across the island to the east. Her hands kneaded together in a tight ball, and her eyes began to mist.

"Damn that's high," she choked out through trembling lips.

"You don't have to, dear," Dad remarked. "We'll all understand if you don't wish to."

She flashed a glance at Jack and then at me. She breathed in heavily again. Blinking repeatedly and quickly, she swallowed hard.

"I'll do it."

CHAPTER 17

Darkness overtook our campground and a flickering fire crackled in the fire pit. The six of us sat around it, snacking, hydrating, and generally resting our weary joints. Ben toasted a marshmallow in the fire, dangling the gooey treat above the flames on a sharp stick.

"I have an idea," Dad began. "What if we each take turns telling a story? It's a grand tradition of campers everywhere."

"Gay," Jack replied.

"Shut up," Erin quickly fired back.

"Let's do it," Ben said with vigor in his voice.

"Okay then, who would like to go first?" Dad inched forward, pushing a piece of driftwood over in the flames with his boot.

"I'll go," Ben volunteered. "I have a good story."

We adjusted our positions around the fire. Ben improved his posture as the rest of us rested comfortably under blankets or in sleeping bags.

"I was climbing this ridge in Vermont. I went by myself because I wanted the challenge. This ridge shot high into the air, almost straight up, kind of like what we have to climb tomorrow. Anyway, it was starting to get later in the day and I still had some distance to go before I reached an area where I could camp.

I tied in at this one rock and prepared to push up to my next foothold when I heard this shrill cry on the wind. It didn't sound like an animal cry; it was higher and louder. I wasn't prepared for the noise, and it sent a shiver down my spine. I stopped my progress and tried to look around me, to see if I could find the source of the noise. I couldn't find anything.

"I let the fright in my body subside and pressed on. A few minutes later, the cry rang out again. It sounded closer this time, even louder than before. I pressed close to the rocks and banged against them with my equipment. I clanked clamps against the rock, trying to scare the source of the noise away with noise of my own. The call dragged on for a longer time than before, but then it ceased again. I stayed still for a few more minutes then pushed myself up higher once more.

"Well, an hour clicked by, and my climb had slowed to little more than inching up the wall. The sun had almost exhausted itself on the horizon, and I picked my way up the rock carefully. I needed to get another twenty or so feet up this cliff before I reached a flat spot where I could camp.

"Suddenly, the cry came again. This time, it seemed on top of me. The high pierced squeal shook me, it felt that close. I ignored safety at that point, scrambling up the rock without regard for my own well being. Whatever was making that noise, it showed a great deal of interest in me. I wanted nothing to do with it.

"I reached the plateau and quickly built a circle of fire, which I sat inside. The wailing continued for a long time, more than fifteen minutes. It sounded like no animal I ever encountered in any setting. It was more guttural than a moose, louder than an elk, and more fearsome than a bear. Whatever stalked me, it seemed angry for some reason. I shuddered within the circle with a pile of rocks by my side. I'd hear the noise and fire a rock in that direction. The noise would cease briefly, but soon would return.

"The night dragged on slowly, and I struggled to keep the fire going around me. I felt no need for sleep, mainly because fear took over and didn't allow fatigue to set in. What sparse trees surrounded me provided little protection for me and a great deal of cover for whatever it was that was out there. I sat there, paranoid, fearing for my life.

"Then I saw what I can't forget. Two yellow eyes glowed from the tree line, off to my right. At first I didn't see them because they were out of my line of sight. When I turned, I was met with these eyes. I began to kick the dirt around me and yell at the top of my lungs. I picked up rock after rock and threw them into the trees near these eyes. The thing stood there, watching.

"Then it let out one huge growl and the eyes flickered out. I heard limbs snapping, the sound of them growing fainter. One final cry shrieked out in the distance then the creature was gone.

"From that day forward, I climb with another person. I won't be caught alone with another creature like that one."

"That really happen?" I asked, in a hushed voice.

"Yes," Ben replied.

"Shit, Dewey," Jack remarked. "You saw Bigfoot."

"I don't know that. I never found out what it was."

"Good story, Ben," Dad said. "Who's next?"

"I'll go next," Jack said.

Jack cleared his throat and patted his hands together before speaking. "Before I begin, let me make sure you all know this story is completely true. Everything I tell you happened.

"And it happened right here, twenty years ago."

We all groaned at his sentence.

"How's this go? Oh yes. Once these three Asian brothers took a rowboat out here to the island from the shore. It was just after graduation from college for the youngest and they wanted to celebrate the fact that he had earned his diploma. Also, the holidays approached and they wanted to be together. They came here, weighed down with sake and Green Teas and whatever the fuck those kids drink.

"They didn't anticipate the rough water offshore, and their rowboat soon flipped over. They saved their alcohol and what little else they could salvage and worked their way to shore. Stranded, and before the time of cell phones, the three brothers huddled together, frightened that they were going to die here.

"The oldest brother, Chien, suffered through the first night with hypothermia and soon fell into unconsciousness. His two brothers, Xien and Bien, tried to keep him alive throughout the day, but Chien died during the second afternoon. His two brothers mourned him as they struggled to survive themselves.

"These brothers came from the city and had no idea about survival skills. They couldn't even figure out how to catch fish or dig for clams. Their hunger grew and grew, and all they had was their beverages, a knife, and Chien's dead body.

"On the third day, they couldn't take it no more. They needed to eat. They looked at each other and discussed what they had to do. After a long argument, the youngest, Bien, made the tough decision. They built a fire, gutted their brother, carved him up, and ate his flesh.

"The next day, Xien took a turn for the worse. He fell while looking for food on the island and fractured his skull. He struggled for life in the surf, but he, too, died.

"Bien was left alone, and he cried and cried on this very beach. He wished he could take the place of both his brothers, and as night fell on the fifth day, he began nibbling at Xien, having exhausted the useful portions of Chien. Two more days, then Bien ran out of wine, water, and Xien. Tired of the pain, forever scarred from the experience, he climbed that rock and jumped from it.

"The next day, a Coast Guard cutter arrived and found the grisly scene. They found half of Chien and Xien and the shattered corpse of Bien. They quietly cleaned up the tragic scene. However, a reporter uncovered the story and wrote of it. The story appeared in the next day's paper.

"And the headline read: Ho, Ho, Ho."

"Shit," I groaned. "All that for a horrible joke."

Jack laughed uncontrollably. "Got all of you."

"My turn," I said, trying to diffuse the momentum Jack had built up with his awful tale.

"Once there was a lighthouse that sat next to the sea. This lighthouse watched the water from the point. It was a cheerful creature, painted like a barber's pole, red and white. But it was lonely by itself on the point.

"One day a man arrived. He wore a long rain slicker and carried a duffel bag. He came to the lighthouse and opened his door. The man settled in and struck up a friendship with the lighthouse. They seemed the perfect match, the thoughtful man and his trusty companion.

"The man and the lighthouse grew older together. Over the next few years, the man's dark beard thickened and his care for the lighthouse increased as well. He always kept the lighthouse clean both outside and in. He changed the light in the tower often and kept a careful watch over the ocean, making sure all vessels out there passed by the lighthouse in safety. No ships ever crashed against the rocks under the careful watch of the keeper.

"Soon enough, the keeper was joined by another human. This woman first showed up in the heat of summer. Her reddish hair cascaded down from her head. The keeper held her close and she returned his comforting embrace. They walked the grounds together, hand in hand, day after day. Their combined lust for life filled the lighthouse with a warm glow.

"The lighthouse was never happier than the day he got to see his best friend get married. The lighthouse stood watch over the proceedings as the keeper in his black suit and the woman in her white dress met on the edge of the point. A third man carrying a thick book spoke words to the couple over the pounding of the surf below them. They exchanged rings then turned to meet the clapping of other people who sat on the grounds. They kissed and the lighthouse smiled. His master smiled back. All was right with the world.

"Over the next few years, the couple roamed the grounds. They'd disappear for a few days at a time then show up again to visit. While they were gone, another keeper busied himself with the task of operating the lighthouse. The lighthouse liked him too, just not as much as his original master. This second keeper didn't keep as careful a lighthouse. The paint started to fade and mildew began to build on the lighthouse's sides. His lamp grew older and the windows in the tower cracked in places. The lighthouse didn't mind, for growing old was part of life, and the lighthouse had already lived a healthy existence.

"One night the lighthouse's favorite master was there, but without his wife. The keeper's face constantly frowned. 'Don't worry old friend,' he said, 'we're going to be okay.' The lighthouse tried to comfort his keeper as best he could, with the warm embrace of his inner tower. The keeper cried at his post in the observation deck.

"The sea swirled with a storm that night, a rough storm that tossed the water about frantically. The lighthouse worked hard, straining his beam of light deep into the torrent. His beam passed over the ocean and swept over the land. When it returned to the water, it flashed on a ship that approached the rocks below. The ship came in hard and fast and couldn't turn in time. The keeper rang the horn into the night and trained the lamp on the ship, but it was too late. The ship slammed headlong into the rocks, breaking apart on impact. The keeper screamed to God for forgiveness and buried his head in his hands. The lighthouse said a separate prayer, hoping that the passengers on the vessel would be okay.

"Morning dawned and the wreckage washed ashore on the beach below. The lighthouse dripped tears as it looked over what had happened. He watched his keeper wander in the surf below, investigating what remained of the ship. The ship wasn't a trawler or an industrial vessel. It was meant to carry people from one point to the other. The keeper sifted through what he found, then stopped cold when he found a crumpled heap on the sand.

"The lighthouse watched his master drop to his knees beside the lifeless body sprawled face down on the beach. The man bellowed loudly, then scooped up the body and carried it back to the lighthouse. The lighthouse looked down when the keeper reached the grounds, and saw the body of the keeper's wife in his keeper's arms.

"As darkness fell, the keeper and the lighthouse buried the keeper's wife. They constructed a cross from pieces of the ship itself and marked where they buried her. The keeper cried without end, and the lighthouse prayed for his forgiveness for not seeing the boat in time.

"That night, the sea crackled again. A deluge of rain poured in sheets from the sky. The waves crashed against the point and the sea rolled over itself multiple times. The lighthouse held fast against a constant strong wind and heard a commotion coming from within its tower.

"Its master appeared on the observation deck. His eyes were swollen red and his shoulders were slumped. He looked out over the sea through the window then backed up toward the lamp. The keeper fired a clear bottle into the lamp, which exploded in a shower of sparks. The keeper wailed in anguish as he stumbled through the darkness and down the staircase. A hollow echo sounded his exit. That was the last time anyone set foot within the lighthouse.

"A lighthouse stands on a lonely point above the sea. Its paint has faded from the color and design of a barber's pole to a pale runny swirl of red and white. Rust colored stains run along its sides. A window is broken in the tower, and the door is padlocked shut. If you listen closely, especially late at night, you can almost hear the lighthouse, asking for forgiveness, crying in the night."

"Well done, Pickle." Dad smiled proudly. Erin rubbed moisture from her eyes.

"Thanks. Tanner, your turn."

"Okay. My story isn't as sad as yours but it is true. Wait, it is pretty sad. Anyway, here goes.

"I once had a German shepherd named Merlin. We got Merlin when I was three. I loved that dog. He'd always want to play and would follow me everywhere.

"One winter afternoon when I was nine, my cousins and I were playing on the frozen pond at my grandparents' house. We had a huge snowball fight earlier, but now we were skating on the ice. We played three on three hockey on the pond, shooting pucks at each other when we stayed upright. Merlin chased us up and down the ice, occasionally tripping one of us up. I told Merlin to lie down on the side of the pond, and he obediently did so.

"Anyway, my cousin Gregg shot the puck behind one of the goals we'd set up, out onto part of the pond we chose not to use. I carelessly skated out to where the puck had stopped. I heard a strange crunching sound beneath me, and I frantically tried to turn and get off the ice.

"Before I could do so, the ice gave way and I fell through. Let me tell you, you've never felt pain like when you fall into a frozen over stretch of water. The water cuts into you like a million knives. It hurts so bad you forget to remember. I bobbed back to the surface luckily and immediately thrashed about, trying to scream for help.

"I couldn't get a grip on anything, and what was worse, my clothes were beginning to weigh me down. My winter clothing was pulling me under. I swung my arms wildly, trying with all my might to gain a hold of anything. There was nothing but the ice to try to grab. I screamed and screamed, but nobody could come out to help me without risking falling in themselves.

"My head went under again and I couldn't seem to get it back above the water. Oh my God, I thought, I'm going to die. I forced my head above water again and gulped in what air I could. Once more, my head went under. I was a goner.

"From under the water, I heard a splash near me. Merlin's face entered my sight. His jaws snapped over my collar and that dog lifted me up with whatever strength it had inside. I gulped air again as Merlin slipped below the surface and under me. I pushed myself up off his back and found my way out of the water.

"My relatives rushed to my side with quilts to warm me. I could do little more than lay alongside the hole in the ice. I waited for Merlin to reappear at the surface. Two minutes. Three minutes. Nothing.

"Later that day, my grandfather cut through the ice and pulled Merlin's body from the pond. The poor dog drowned saving me. My most loyal friend gave his life so I could live some more.

When I finally get to heaven, the first thing I'm doing is finding Merlin to thank him."

Now we were all sniffling. Even Jack found it hard to keep a macho facade up in the face of that story.

"Do you have a story, Erin?" Dad asked under the shadows and flickering flames. He poked a stick at the limbs in the fire, trying to fan the embers further.

"You go ahead, Dr. McCracken," she replied. In the darkness, I saw her eyes shifting back and forth, between me and Jack, never resting on either one of us for more than a couple seconds. I turned to Dad.

"Yes, Dad," I added, "please tell us something."

"Okay," he started, "but my story probably won't compare to you guys' tales. I'll do my best.

"Once, when I was only about thirteen, I was visiting with my father in northern France. My father knew a couple archaeologists there and we went across the channel for the weekend so Father could confer with them about a lead he wanted to explore. We arrived on a Friday under the cover of a dense fog and slight drizzle.

"The two gentlemen met us when our ship arrived and immediately took us out to a remote beach on the coast. We arrived after dark and found a place to spend the night. I went to sleep as Father talked with his French colleagues, planning the attempt.

"The following morning, we awoke early and set out for a high point along the coastline. Father and his French friends discussed the hopes they shared for the adventure as we slowly trekked up the slope and to a small cave, hidden among a series of boulders and from view. How they knew where to go I don't know for sure. We quickly scoured the outer opening before venturing inside.

"The cave was darker than it should have been. The walls felt like they were covered with slime, and the air stank with a kind of musk. There were some drawings on the walls near the entrance, but as we ventured deeper into this cavern, the rock drawings ceased. We carried torches, the four of us. The two Frenchmen led the way, and Father and I followed behind. The cavern grew tighter and tougher to navigate.

"We crawled through this opening in the wall, and when we emerged on the other side, the cave was bathed in a faint glow. It was the most bizarre thing I had seen in my young life. For some reason, yellow light existed where no light should possibly be. We found ourselves in a large chamber, nearly circular in shape and immense. And in the center of the room, on a high platform, a dozen golden cups rested.

"Dad cautioned the Frenchmen to keep their distance, to refrain from touching anything until he inspected the cups further. Father explained to us that the first three cups must be removed in the proper order before the other nine could be taken. According to legend, the Twelve Chalices of Athena represented the twelve symbols of the zodiac, and disturbing them without the correct procedure meant certain doom for the unfortunate souls involved. The French duo listened, thank goodness, and Father stepped to the platform, to decipher the order the cups should be removed.

"Father immediately stepped to a thick cup, one that had matching handles on either side. The two handles were identical and were linked just under the lip of the chalice by a band of gold encrusted with grand jewels. It had two separate halves that could hold water. 'This is the Chalice of the Gemini,' Father proclaimed. 'It is the chalice of the renewal of life.' With that, he carefully lifted it from the platform and handed it behind himself to me.

"He wiped sweat from his brow and slowly stepped around the circle counterclockwise, six cups from where he started. The next chalice he stopped at resembled a water pitcher; it stood higher than all the other relics in the circle. The chalice had one handle, intricately carved and shaped like a crescent moon. 'This is the Chalice of Sagittarius,' Father announced. 'It is the chalice of the celebration of life.' With that, he lifted it from the platform and handed it to me.

"He squinted in the darkness, looking across the circle from his position. He backtracked clockwise around the circle, stopping three more chalices away from his last stop. He ground his fingers together, looking at the cup before him.

"The cup before him was little more than a straight drinking cup. It shone brightly, completely detailed in gold. Father breathed in slowly then placed his hands on the platform in front of the chalice. 'This is the Chalice of Virgo,' he said. 'It is the chalice of the miracle of life.' He put his hands around the cup, picked it up from the platform, and handed it to me as well.

"As I grabbed it, I inspected it for the first time. The Chalice of Virgo was solid. It possessed no opening. In other words, the Chalice of Virgo wasn't meant for liquid consumption, because it was nothing more than a solid piece of material, with no place for water to be held.

"After Father handed me the third chalice, the French duo quickly collected the remaining nine chalices. We sacked them up and vacated the cave. To this day, those twelve relics that prove the

Greek empire reached into Western Europe remain in a collection in a museum in Paris.

"That was the first time I went on an adventure and discovered a priceless relic. To this day, it ranks as one of my greatest highlights of life."

"You found a cup that wasn't a cup at all?" Jack asked.

"Yes son, I did."

"That's the weirdest thing I've ever heard of."

Dad scratched his head for a moment, then lifted his glasses and rubbed his right eye.

"Now it's your turn, dear," Dad said to Erin. "Do you have a story for us?"

She looked over at me for a moment. She glanced up and down at me before speaking.

"I…sure do." She breathed in deeply with her hesitation.

"There was once this fair maiden that lived in a grand land. She was adored by a handsome prince and was to be married to him. She thought that this prince was to be her life, that she would serve him loyally and all would be right. However, she wasn't happy.

"This prince showed her affection, but only when he felt it fit. When he thought it was right, they would join together as one. When not, he would belittle her or ignore her and tease the other maidens in the castle. Meanwhile, his brother, the first in line for the throne, calmly went about the business of being her friend.

"She'd known the older prince almost her entire life. They grew up together on the castle grounds, frolicking through the royal gardens and tormenting the handmaidens and knights with their tricks. They liked each other as friends, but never showed more of a connection than that. When the maiden became promised to the younger prince, the elder offered his undying support to both of them.

"One night, the maiden walked the castle courtyard alone. As she wandered through the night, she happened upon the older prince, standing by himself in the moonlight. He stared skyward, oblivious to her presence, until she reached out and touched him.

"'I did not see you there fair maiden,' he said. 'Wilst thou join me?'

"'Yes my lord,' she replied.

"She wandered over him with her eyes, noticing that he seemed to be in great pain. 'What troubles you?' she asked.

"'I wish you were two. That way, I'd be able to have one of my own.'

"She stood back in shock, not knowing what to think. He raised her chin with his hand and looked deeply into her eyes.

"She closed her eyes and allowed the older prince to kiss her. The kiss lasted but a few seconds, but it felt so right that it seemed to have no limit in time. The kiss seemed to exist in a different plane of love than any other type of kiss, for it came from somebody that the maiden had waited her entire life to find. A kiss between two true loves outdistances anything that happens between any other two people, for it comes from true love. As the kiss ended, the maiden was left to wonder what to do."

Erin pushed herself back to a slouched position. She kept her eyes on me the whole time. I swallowed hard as I listened to her story end.

"So," Jack asked, "what happened next?"

Erin looked into the fire. "She let the fates decide." She stood to her feet and left the circle, ducking into her tent.

I drummed my fingers on my legs. Jack punched his right fist into his left hand.

"I'm going to bed," Jack announced to the group.

"Me too," I added.

"Good idea," Dad muttered. "Good night everyone."

We all dispersed from beside the fire. Tanner doused the flame before following us to camp. He stopped for a moment in the low moonlight, glanced up at Serpent Rock, and disappeared into our tent.

CHAPTER 18

I awoke with a start as Tanner sawed logs in his sleeping bag. Flashing a glance at my watch, I muttered a profanity at Tanner, cursing his incessant snoring. I rolled toward the flap of the tent and stumbled into the night air again.

For the second straight night, I wandered down to the water's edge and watched the sea crash together for awhile. Under the moonlight, the sea appeared white. The moon's reflection bobbed in the water, being tossed about, bouncing up and down on the crests of the waves that approached the beach. I stood stationary at the water's edge, letting my cares float away on the water.

A shadow invaded my spot, coming from behind me and overtaking my feet. I looked down first then turned slowly over my right shoulder to see who was joining me this evening. As Erin stepped toward me, I swallowed hard in anticipation of what this encounter would bring.

I noticed something about her for the first time that night that I hadn't before. Her eyelids were puffy and tired, her hair a tangled, matted nest, and her mouth a droopy, sleepy, heavy mouth, yet she still looked beautiful. Some women look spectacular with primping, make-up, and careful care for themselves, but when all the exterior stuff has been removed they don't look nearly as good. However, Erin wasn't like that. She wore no foundation or eye shadow, no intricate hairstyle, no expensive clothes. Yet, in her simple way, I found her to be the most beautiful creation on God's Earth, without all the covering most people felt they needed to present themselves as attractive to the public. Sure she had little choice at the time, but still the fact remained that I realized how naturally devastatingly beautiful she was, right then. Erin could live forever in gray sweatpants, a powder blue long sleeved shirt, and white Keds, and I would forever bow in the midst of her beauty. No matter what, she would always be the one that I had looked for my entire life, whether I earned her hand or not.

I waited with baited breath for her to speak to me.

"Hey," she whispered.

"Hey," I whispered back.

"Listen, I hope you understood my story tonight."

"I think I did."

"So...since it's the case...um, what do you think?"

In my head, I told her everything. I talked to her about how I'd wanted her my entire life, how every move I'd made in life was in search of her. All the false starts I'd made with others were mere preparation for The One, the person who would share my dreams and, in many cases, either fulfill or create them. I wanted to remind her of how all the women I'd attempted a relationship with looked like her in at least some respects, and how all the best in them added up to her. I thought about how I always felt safe with her, how no matter what happened in my life, no matter how down I got on myself, no matter how many disappointments befell me, it all melted away in her presence. She was the reason for me to live. Erin Lomansky was life itself.

"I don't know," I softly remarked.

"What were you thinking when you kissed me last night?" she asked me.

"I really wasn't. At first. When it happened, I only thought of what I wanted to do. I wanted you."

"And now?"

"Same thing." I leaned in to her and touched her cheeks with my hands. I pulled her face closer, and as I closed my eyes, I pressed my lips to hers.

After a few seconds, I backed out of the smooch. I took a shallow breath. Erin allowed me the air intake, then leaned in and kissed me. This kiss lasted longer. It wasn't a friendly peck, and it wasn't a passionate prelude to intercourse. This kiss represented the best that mankind can create, a bond between two people who are perfect for each other. The rest of the world would fade away in light of such a kiss. Any person engaged in this type of kiss lost touch with the physical realm and entered a spiritual plane reserved for those few who are truly blessed, those few who got to feel the magic of such a kiss. As the world disappeared into the background, I accepted the caress of Erin's lips with mine, and I pulled her closer, promising with my arms to never let go.

We lowered to the sand's surface and rested on our sides. The kissing between us grew more aggressive, and we rolled in the sand as we took turns expressing our feelings. Nothing more than kissing occurred, mainly because at this point nothing else mattered. It was hard to speak for Erin, but I knew without a doubt that what we shared was right. No matter what the circumstance, this kiss meant everything, as this kiss came from two true hearts. As we made out under the moon's loving gaze, we continued to show each other how the other meant the world.

I opened my eyes just before Erin did the same. We continued to kiss, but now we made eye contact. She faced the camp while my back was turned to it. I watched her brilliant hazel eyes shimmer in the moonlight and glanced at her glowing strawberry blonde hair. Our limbs intertwined as we embraced on the beach. Then, without warning, she stopped and rolled away from me.

I was pushed face down in the sand and couldn't move. Blows rained down on me from behind, impacting me between my shoulder blades and my kidneys, repeatedly and in no discernible pattern. My arms were pinned at my sides, trapped there by my unseen attacker. Shots continued down on me from behind, and I couldn't defend myself. I heard cries of help from Erin and a stream of profanity from my assailant, but their words melted together in a clump of gibberish as they entered my ears. My face was buried in the sand, and I choked as I swallowed the salty grains. Then, just as suddenly as the attack began, it stopped.

I rolled from my stomach to my back, struggling to catch the breath that had been beaten from me. My ribs ached from the blows, and I rose to a seated position to try to help them. I looked to my left and caught a glimpse of my attacker for the first time as he cursed me in a rushed voice.

"Motherfucker! What the fuck!" Jack's face raged with anger, his fists balled with despair. He wanted to jump me again, but he fought in the arms of Ben, ankle deep in the water. Erin pleaded with him off to his left, bawling uncontrollably and shaking. I made it to my feet and tried to walk off the pain.

"You sorry son of a bitch!" Jack yelled at me. Even in the pale moonlight, I could see the flushed shade in his face.

I waved him off with my left hand as Dad reached me.

"You okay, Pickle?" he asked. He tried to clasp my shoulder, but I shrugged him away.

"Is he okay? What the fuck is this!"

"Calm down, son," Dad calmly requested. He took a timid step toward Jack.

"Fuck that, Seamus!"

Dad stopped dead in his tracks. "What did you call me, son?"

"Your name, you old fuck. You're not my dad."

"No Jack, I am. Now come here please."

"NO! Leave me be!" Jack stormed past Dad and toward the underbrush at the trail head. He picked up a stick and proceeded to

beat the ground repeatedly with the branch.
Dad grabbed Erin and held her tight. She sobbed loudly in his embrace. Tears glistened in the moonlight off her face. Her eyes flooded with the tears, which slid in a steady stream from her ducts. She tried to form words, but all that came out were a series of incoherent wailing consonants.
"Guys," Ben grunted. "Guys. Help."
Ben dropped to his right knee in the sand. He clutched at his right wrist with his left hand. He was doubled over in pain, curling his body over the wounded area. He forced air through his gritted teeth as he tried to figure out how to lessen the searing pain that rushed up his arm.
"What happened? Dewey?" I rushed over to him.
"When I tackled him, we both landed with our weight on my arm. I don't think it's broken. It just sort of buckled under me."
I inspected his wrist in the moonlight. Swelling and discoloration already spread over the injured area.
"Dad? Dad, we need to take care of Dewey. It doesn't look good."
Dad released Erin, who ran into the darkness. He lifted Ben to his feet and helped him to camp. I watched the whole scene unfold before me before stomping to my shelter.
I threw myself into my tent and kicked my sleeping bag. As I slammed fists into my pillows, I looked over at Tanner. He continued to sleep, loudly snoring, oblivious to everything that blew up outside the camp. I cursed him and tossed in my slumber bag for the remainder of the night.

CHAPTER 19

I awoke before dawn the next day. More accurately, I never slept that night. June twenty-first began earlier than any other day of the year, being the summer solstice. The way I understood it, the farther north you went the longer the day became. We were about halfway up the northern hemisphere on Baffert Island as the solstice commenced.

I snacked on a Fruit Roll-Up at the trailhead, staring over the abyss of the island's interior, the vast field of lush greenery that covered the expanse. Stupid Jack and his idea of a balanced breakfast. I stayed there alone, in the fading darkness, until a second individual strode up beside me.

"Morning," Erin yawned. She carried a blanket over her shoulders. Even without make-up on, even in her disheveled state, even with squinted eyes and puffy eyelids, I still found her more attractive than any woman I'd ever met, known, or seen.

"Sorry," I replied.

"Are you really?" she retorted. She carried concern, not anger, in her voice. She attempted to knock the sleep from her corneas by trying to force them wide.

"I've thought about this all night. It was wrong to cheat Jack like I did." My voice trailed off as I finished my sentence.

"I know..."

"Let me finish. Please." I breathed in softly. "It was wrong to cheat Jack, but it's even more wrong to cheat myself. If I'm not with you, I'm cheating myself out of the happiness I deserve. And you're cheating yourself as well."

"I...I...don't know."

I placed my hand on her shoulder. "I don't expect you to. Just know I'm here. I know we're going to make it. Take your time and figure out what's best. We'll both be better off when you stop asking 'Why' and start saying 'Why not'. No matter what, I'll be here when you decide."

"Thanks, Jared. I hope Jack feels the same."

I hoped he wouldn't.

Erin backed away from me. She stopped as she began to wander down the shallow incline to the camp.

"Jared?"

"Yes Erin."

"I almost forgot. Happy Birthday."

"Thanks." I had nearly forgotten as well. After all, my nineteenth birthday began with me receiving a vicious beating. I wondered what other gifts might materialize as I chewed my sheet of cherry flavor. I remained in the same spot, at the trailhead, deciding to wait for the sun to rise.

Dad showed up as the sun started to lift into the sky. "Sol has the long shift today," he said as he broke stride.

"Morning, Dad."

"How's nineteen feel, Pickle?"

"So far it kind of hurts." I cast my eyes to the earth.

"Don't worry about Jack. He'll recover."

"But Dad, I'm the cause of the problem."

"Son, all problems manifest themselves from multiple beginnings. The thought that you're the sole cause is ludicrous. Every person that took part in that situation last night shares the blame."

I looked up again. "I guess so." The shame in my soul seeped out of me into the dawn. I refused to try to hold it in. My shame filled the air with a stench that carried on the breeze and into the valley before me.

Dad rubbed his eye under his glasses as he continued. "Now don't worry about it. We need you in the game today, more than ever. Without you, this won't work."

"I understand." I paused for a moment, thinking of what to say next.

"Dad," I said, "I hope we find it today."

"Me too, son. Me too."

"Dad? Do you ever regret me?"

Dad furrowed his brow at the question. "No. Why do you ask?"

My lip began to quiver as I spoke. "Well, you know, nineteen years ago today, Mom left the world behind."

"Son, I know you blame yourself. You can't. That day, when your mother left for the eternal, I lost a great companion. However, I would never trade what I've lost for what I have. Son, I have never regretted you."

"But Dad," I whimpered, "I…I killed her."

For some strange reason, the tears that should have fallen freely refused to slip from my eyes. They hung there, fogging my vision with a slick liquid film. I ducked my head into Dad's chest and let him hold me.

"Don't say that, son," he pleaded. "You can't think that. If it wasn't for you, I don't know how my life would've turned out. It's you that makes me proud. It's not everything I've done, it's not my job. It's certainly not finding some new discovery nobody ever heard of but me. My whole life is a success because you are here.

"I could die tomorrow, and I would not regret anything, because I would die knowing that the son I raised was a great man. You didn't kill her, Pickle. You blessed me. It was God's plan, and I've never questioned him for what he decrees."

I stayed in my Dad's embrace as he talked to me. As I rested my head in his loving arms, I felt a warm moist drop trickle down my ear. I heard a faint sniffle, and I relinquished my grip with my father.

The two of us stood there, silent, as the sun emerged from behind the far bluff. Rays of light curved around Serpent Rock first, followed closely by the glowing orb of light. The sun rose straight up in the sky, directly over the promontory that resembled the snake. Once it burst free from behind the rock, the sun immediately bathed the crater floor in luminescence. I squinted under the bright light. It was the brightest I'd ever seen the sun be.

"It came over the serpent!" Dad exclaimed. He hopped once. "Just like I hoped!"

Dad grabbed me at the biceps and started to dance around me in a circle, pulling me with him. "Son! We found it. We found it!" He let out a jubilant holler and bounded down the slope from our position. He continued to call out "We found it!" as he ran down to the camp. I watched him scramble around the campground in glee, and I chuckled softly as I saw him hug each person in turn, even Jack, who sat by himself against a rock with his head down and his hands clutching around his ears. Ben smiled at me as he climbed to my position.

"How's the hand?" I asked.

Ben carried a water bottle on his right wrist. He gingerly removed the bottle, held there to help alleviate the swelling. Twisting the injured joint slowly and wincing during the effort, he mumbled, "It's okay. I'll live."

"But can you climb?"

"We'll see when we get there." He rubbed the injured area against his stomach before reapplying the canteen. "I'm going to tape it up with some duct tape from my pack. Maybe that'll help."

"I hope so. I wouldn't want you to miss it."

"Don't worry, I wouldn't dare. You know, Dwight Evans once rolled over on his wrist, then had a twelve game hitting streak while he waited for it to heal."

I patted him on the shoulder, and the two of us left our perch behind, joining the rest of our crew at our camp.

CHAPTER 20

"Seamus, take a look at this." Tanner sat Indian style on the ground with a portable computer in his lap. He punched keys on the keyboard, which pulled up a series of charts on the screen. "You see this here?"

Dad peered at the screen over his left shoulder. "Yes, Tanner."

Tanner pressed his left index finger against the screen. "This right here?"

"What does it mean, Tanner?"

"Well, as you can see, the earthquakes are intensifying in strength and frequency. This can only mean one thing."

"What's that?"

"This volcano is more active than we thought."

Dad rushed his hand through his thinning hair. "How active, Tanner? Should we leave?"

Tanner scratched his nose. "No...I...think we'll be safe for today. It may be just a cycle the island's suffering. I can't imagine this place erupting this soon."

"So we go then?"

Tanner hesitated in quiet. "Yes, Seamus. Let's do it."

Dad flipped the cell phone from his pocket and punched the proper numbers into it. With quick words, he instructed Mullet Joe to bring Whirlygirl. Dad hung up the phone and pushed it back into his pocket.

"We go," he said.

Instantly, Ben and I rushed forth and hastily started assembling the equipment we'd need. Ben told me what to grab and I piled it beside him on the ground. Ropes, metal pins, clamps, and climbing axes joined the pile. Erin helped as well, while Dad and Tanner inspected a map, huddled together in a far corner. Jack remained fixed to his spot on the log, his face buried in his hands.

We all stopped in our tracks when the flying beast stormed in off the horizon. A small plume belched from her rear rotary blade. The craft came in sideways, settling on the beach with a whirlwind of dust.

Mullet Joe emerged from the cockpit as the blades slowly stopped spinning. "Let me understand you correctly," he yelled over the whining of the blades over head. "You want me to fly you up to the big rock on the other side of the island."

"Yes," Dad replied. "Will that be a problem?"

"I'm not sure yet. I know we can get close, but I may need you to get to the ground without me. I'm not sure of the clearance up there."

"We can handle it," Dad assured him.

Mullet Joe tugged forward on the collar of a pitted out undershirt and burped. He instructed us to load our gear, a moot point since we already attacked the task. Ben led the charge despite his injured wrist, telling us where certain equipment should be placed within the aircraft. We quickly filled the helicopter with our necessary accessories and loaded ourselves into the fuselage.

"Come on Jack," I called as I strapped myself in.

He was slow to show response, lifting his head from his intense stare into the earth after a few seconds. He waved his hand at us in disgust.

I unstrapped myself from my seat and tore the headset from my skull. "Start the engines!" I barked to Mullet Joe as I stomped across the beachhead to Jack.

"What's wrong with you?" I bellowed.

"Fuck off," he replied.

"Get your sorry ass in the chopper now!" I bent down to make eye contact with him. I forced my face in with his.

"Get out of my face!" he growled. His hand flashed out at me, shoving me back a step.

"I will when you get in the goddamn helicopter!" I stepped forward and shoved him back. He looked up, startled that I dared touch him.

He rose to his feet. "We're not through. Not by a long shot." He barked the words to me as he passed me on his way to Whirlygirl. I followed closely and shut the sliding partition behind us as we boarded the helicopter.

The rotors purred to life, filling the surrounding landscape with a gently rising whine. The two blades spun faster until they reached their maximum revolutions per minute. Mullet Joe nudged back the stick, and the war machine lifted off the ground. It rose above the tallest crag on the island then pitched to the right, heading toward an eastern course. Our next stop: Serpent Rock.

CHAPTER 21

Our group sat silent as Whirlygirl climbed into the air, through the steam coming off the lava dome and over the volcanic crater below. Her constantly whirring blades provided the only noise as each of us took in faint breaths and remained inaudible to the others. I for one wondered what awaited us as we approached the drop zone, the plateau of Serpent Rock.

I rubbed a filmy sweat from my palms by running my thumbs across the surface repeatedly. I found it difficult to relax in the bumpy craft, choosing instead to keep an intense stare out the small window to my right. The constant jerking motion of the helicopter on the cross breeze caused me to grasp the front edge of my seat with both hands. I shifted my weight, trying to gain control of something that I had no say over.

I tried to focus on something else as we continued to soar into the heavens. For a time, I mentally hummed "Happy Birthday" in my head. That distraction worked for a short period before I glanced out the window again and returned to the reality of the situation. I tried to tell myself jokes in my head, but they only served to annoy me with their tired punch lines. At one point, I thought I would count the trees on the island, but that plan soon derailed itself when I remembered that the island had no trees. Mostly, I just tried to keep my mind occupied as the nervousness attempted to invade me.

Erin drummed her fingers on her legs as she sat rigidly in her chair. Her face was ashen and the ends of her digits appeared without color. She adjusted a handkerchief she wore over her forehead, a green number folded into a headband that served to hold her hair from her face. I looked at her and she flashed me a lopsided grin that subsided against her nauseous demeanor.

Ben looked like a puppy on a long car ride. He seemed to want to shove his head out the window, to feel the rushing air in his hair and ears as we flew along. He had lightly tinted sunglasses over his eyes, small oval frames that hardly hid the gleam of excitement in his eye. His right wrist was bound tight with black electrician's tape. Upon instant glance, one could see how swollen the joint was.

Jack kept his eyes closed as the flight grew longer. His Red Sox hat remained low over his eyes, and his arms were folded across his chest. An angry scowl decorated his visage. He remained stiff, refusing the urge to find any means of comfort.

Tanner sat with his back to all of us. He wasn't buckled in to any seat; rather, he remained mobile within the fuselage. He stared out the front windshield, his right arm supporting him from its position on the back of Dad's seat in the cockpit. He closely watched our approach.

"I'll take her in low, see if we can land the old girl up there," Mullet Joe crackled through the radio headset. He pushed the stick forward. Suddenly, Whirlygirl lurched forward, her nose diving down with increased speed. Erin whimpered softly when the aircraft began its descent.

I reached over to comfort her. As I went to put my hand on her knee, another hand flashed out from beside me and slapped mine away. I quickly jerked to my left to find Jack, crossing his arms back over his chest. He lowered his head once more and closed his narrow eyes.

The helicopter leveled off and slowed in the sky. I craned my neck to see over Tanner, to see why we hovered in place. Through the windshield, I saw my adversary, Serpent Rock. Its sinister sneer, frozen permanently on its bulbous head, goaded me. I knew it was merely a boulder on top of a ridge, but that didn't stop me from flashing it my middle finger and cursing it silently.

"What're you doing?" Jack asked me, lifting his voice over the rotor blades.

"Nothing," I quickly stammered.

"Dumbass."

I put my hand beside me and nonchalantly flashed him my middle finger from its resting place on my pant leg.

"Dr. McCracken?" Mullet Joe barked over the headset.

"I know, Mr. Cheney. I already know."

Dad wrenched his head around and trained his eyes on us. "Kids, get that rope ready. We're going to have to repel in."

"Yes!" Ben exclaimed. He nearly pulled his arm from the socket trying to leave his seat before uncoupling his belt. He sprang to his feet, not an easy task in the constantly bouncing bowels of Whirlygirl, and slid on his knees to his waiting equipment. "Jared, get that door open!" he ordered while he snapped a vest over his torso.

I thrust open the sliding door of the craft, struggling with it before finally throwing it open. The wind rushed into my face full force, pushing me back for a quick moment. Ben appeared next to me, slipping on a pair of gloves and holding a clamp.

"Attach that line to the winch," he instructed as he performed a quick check of his vest harness. "Everybody, get your vests on. Make sure they're buckled tight or you'll slip right out of them and end up a permanent attraction of this park."

We quickly shrugged the harnesses over our shoulders and buckled them over our chests. Meanwhile, Ben stepped out onto the helicopter skid. He held a length of nylon rope in his left hand and used his swollen right one to slap a clamp connected to his vest over the line.

"I'll secure the line on the ground. Watch me as I drop in, and do exactly as I do. You follow my lead, you'll have no problem. Throw down the other equipment first."

He cupped his left hand over the rope and stepped off the skid. He dangled under the helicopter, the end of the line extending beneath him, flopping like a dying fish on the flat ground below. He slid down the line slowly, using his left hand to direct the rope, his right to hold it against his hip and control the speed of his descent. He slipped to Earth in small spurts, following the procedure of releasing line and lowering at a controlled speed and distance. Ben touched down on land within one minute, softly landing with both feet at once. He waved to us and soon the necessary package of ropes and metal pins impacted the plateau below.

"Start down!" Ben screamed. "I'll hold the line here! Tell Mr. Cheney to winch up the rope once the last person is safely down!"

Dad relayed the message to Mullet Joe as Tanner began his descent. His speed to the ground was much faster than Ben's, and he landed in a heap as he crashed into the surface. Jack chuckled at Tanner's mishap before I nudged him.

"You're next, jackbastard."

Jack buckled in and let out a deafening bellow. He jumped from the craft and slid quickly down the line. Just before reaching solid ground, he tensed his hands on the line, skidding to a stop just short of impact. He let out the line, dropped safely to the ground, released his clamp, and told me to suck it.

"Erin," I called out, "you okay with this?"

She huddled close to the wall opposite the open door. Her face was white.

"Erin?"

"I can't do it! I can't do it!" She sobbed loudly, a violent shake taking over her body. Tears streamed down her face.

"Yes you can," I assured her. I hugged her tight against my body and pecked her on the cheek.

"Erin, it's not bad. Keep your eyes on me as you slide down. Understand?"

She nodded her head and wiped away her stray tears. Erin inched forward to the door and allowed me to secure her clamp over the nylon cable. I helped ease her onto the skid, holding her hand as she stepped out.

Erin let herself off the skid and dangled under the helicopter. She didn't move from that spot. Her grip froze the rope in place, keeping her body swaying under the fuselage.

"Loosen your grip Erin!" Ben called to her.

She looked down between her legs to him. As she did, she spun on the rope. She tightened her legs around the rope and ducked her head into her chest.

"Erin!" I yelled. "Look at me!"

She stayed in a ball, spinning slowly on the nylon cord that extended from helicopter to ground.

"Erin!" I screamed. She didn't respond.

"Dad! Get ready! I'm going now!"

I snapped my clamp on the rope and climbed out of the aircraft. Instead of leaping off, I curled my body around the runner and tried to reach Erin. I couldn't get her from my position.

"Erin! Dammit, look at me!"

Erin kept her chin tucked in her chest. She held her eyes tightly shut. Her shaking caused the rope to vibrate while she spun in a tight circle. The three men on the ground gathered under her.

"She's going to fall!" Jack yelled to me.

I refused to allow it. I lowered myself from the landing runner and slid carefully down to her. She lifted her head when I reached a point just above her.

"Help me Jared! Oh God!"

"I got you! Now listen. I'm going to lower myself outside you. Stay where you are, and don't move!"

She clutched the rope even closer to her, a move I actually wanted her to commit. I kicked my legs wide and slipped behind her.

I jerked to a stop when our twin fasteners struck together.
"I got you! Erin, I got you!"
This was the easy part. The wind picked up, and the helicopter's proximity to the ground, coupled with its extended period of hovering, kicked up dust beneath us. The cloud rose around us as I made my move.
I wrapped a length of cord around my left fist once, to anchor me in place. I tugged it to tighten the loop then let the slack rope in my right hand go free. I slipped my right arm under hers as I grabbed the line again. "Let go with your right hand," I calmly instructed, and Erin released her slack. She still held the rope with her left hand and had her feet intertwined with it. I tangled my feet in the line also, and worked my body under her.
"Now, when I say so, let go with your left hand and grab me."
"NO! I'll fall!"
"Trust me! I won't let you go!"
She sobbed as she gathered the courage. I could feel her heart pounding from my spot behind her. Either this would work or we'd both splatter ourselves on the rocks below.
"On the count of three."
She grunted, which I assumed meant she agreed.
"One." I pushed my body closer to her and down a couple inches. My left hand held the rope fast above me, and my right kept her pinned in the space inside me.
"Two." I tightened my legs around the black nylon. I used my right toe to try and loop a stretch of the cord around my left foot.
I exhaled my air from my lungs, paused, and took in a deep gulp.
"Three."
Time stopped the second Erin released the cable. She twisted her upper body in the air, flipping in a turn to her left. Her right arm caught me over the clavicle and she dug her nails into my T-shirt. Her left hand grasped me over my right shoulder. I thrust my weight up to

DOME OF THE ROCK

meet her and trapped her within my embrace, using my right arm to catch her by tucking it up through her armpit and behind her. She let her legs dangle beneath her for a moment before wrapping them around my right leg. Finally safe, she adjusted her weight and clutched me tightly, interlocking her hands on my back, her right arm over my shoulder, her left under the pit. I allowed the rope to loosen from around my fist and slowly lowered the two of us to the safety of the ground below us.

"Oh my God! Thank you! Thank you!" Erin held me tightly to her as I set us down on the plateau. I unbuckled us from the rope and tossed the rope aside. She collapsed to her knees, in tears, and I walked nine steps before I fell to my knees, succumbing to the fear for her that minutes before caused me to take action. I shook uncontrollably, with my head buried in my hands, in a kneeling position.

Dad repelled down from the sky and waved up at Mullet Joe. The black nylon rope lifted from the ground as it was wound onto the mechanical winch's spool. Mullet Joe waved down to us from the cockpit. Dad returned a gesture, pressing his right forefingers against his brow, extending his hand, and retracting them again. Whirlygirl rose over the crest of the ridge and turned in a northern banking maneuver. Once it was pointed to the west, the helicopter steamed away from us.

"What now?" Tanner asked Dad.

"I think we'll take a short break," he replied.

"Smoke 'em if you got 'em," Jack added. He produced a pack of cigarettes from his chest pocket and pulled one from it. Tanner also reached out and claimed a cigarette. I wouldn't have minded one then myself, but I already lacked breath. Plus, the fear that had overtaken me wouldn't allow me to steady myself enough to operate any type of lighter, match, or even a flaming torch.

At least she was okay.

CHAPTER 22

"Son, what you did back there...incredible."

I looked up through my fatigue to find Dad standing over me.

"Thanks, Dad. It had to be done."

"But not everyone can do something like that. Where did you learn to do that?"

"I didn't learn. Just reacted."

"Incredible." Dad patted me as I continued to breathe deeply, in my kneeling position.

"I'll be fine in a minute. We can continue whenever Erin's ready."

Dad glanced over to the group, standing at the edge of the flat plateau we occupied. "Looks like she already is," he mentioned, pointing to our four companions. Erin stood with the three males, her head lowered slightly but otherwise none the worse for wear. I lifted my weary body from the dust and clapped Dad on the shoulder.

"Let's do this."

We approached as Ben continued to speak to the others. "We'll do the same thing we just did, only this time it will be easier. Having something to put your feet against will make it less dangerous."

"It can't be more," Jack hissed.

"Shut up, Jack," I snapped.

"Oh look, it's mister hero. Well, Erin, maybe you should kiss him now. Oh wait, you already did that."

Erin's tears returned in force and poured from her beautiful hazel eyes.

"Oh, knock it off Erin. I'm sick of you getting away with everything. You think I don't know how big a liar you are!" She swallowed hard. "What?!?"

"Oh, come on. This shit's gotta stop. You're not on the rag, you just want to fuck Jared!"

"Careful bro." I took a step forward.

"And what're you gonna do birthday boy? Huh? You gonna let me kick your ass some more?"

"Shut up!" Erin yelled. "Shut up shut up shut up! Jesus!"

"As for you," Jack remarked, "it's probably a good thing I fucked Cheryl at the party the other night."

Erin stopped crying once those words left Jack's mouth. Time stopped as each of us took in the scope of Jack's words, what they meant. The thoughts of Jack being unfaithful had crossed my mind in the past, but I never believed him actually capable of following through on such a truly despicable action. My mouth dropped open and remained agape, the common bond we all shared, save for Tanner, who could have given a damn less.

Erin's face contorted from one of sadness to one of rage. She took in one breath, leaned back, and punched Jack square in the mouth, a sharp left-handed strike.

Jack rolled with the blow, but he still caught the brunt of the haymaker. He spun on his toe, and when he turned his fists were balled and ready to strike. Jack raised his arm to throw a straight right. He pulled it short when Dad stepped between the two lovers.

"And you," Jack hissed, "my so-called father. Well, fuck you, and fuck this stupid chase. You've almost gotten all of us killed at least once."

Dad listened to the words escape Jack's mouth and scratched his temple. Jack lowered his fists, and when he did so, Dad shoved Jack with twin palm strikes, much like a sumo wrestler would do to win a match. Jack stumbled back before falling to the ground.

"You show the young lady some respect," Dad politely requested. "And when you're ready to grow up, help us. Please. We need you."

Jack rested in the dirt, staying on his backside. He fumed for a second then climbed back to his feet. Refusing to dust himself off, Jack rushed past us and wandered near Serpent Rock. He hastily lit and smoked another cigarette.

That was the first time I saw Dad physically become involved with anyone. Dad believed strongly in solving matters without violence and constantly tried to teach us by example. My mouth hung open when Dad lashed out at Jack. Never before had I seen Dad use force like he did with Jack. I hoped I wouldn't have to see it again.

CHAPTER 23

I guzzled water from my canteen as the sun passed directly over us. I splashed water in my hair and took a handful of the cool liquid to my neck. Replacing my canteen on my belt, I stopped to study what Ben was doing.

Ben laid flat on the edge of the ridge. He kept his palms on solid ground, but his head and neck extended over the cliff and peered down at the sheer face below. He lined up a narrow ledge, no more than three feet in width and twenty feet in length, with himself, scooting along the ground in his prone position. He pushed himself back from the ledge, got to his feet, and drew a cross in the faint dust with his toe. He walked past the group and headed toward his equipment stash.

"Getting down there shouldn't be a problem. That ledge over the cave should suit us just fine."

Ben pulled a device from his duffel bag as he spoke to us from his knees. He opened a plastic carrying case, snapping open two bolts to lift the lid. He fished inside the case as he talked.

"This gun here will help us," he explained. "It's a piton gun. I can load it with these pins and fire them into the bedrock. Once the pins are secure, we'll have the support we need."

"How's it work, Dewey?" Erin asked. She gently stroked the knuckles that moments before had collided with her boyfriend's cheating jaw.

"Simple, Erin," Ben said. "The pin goes in the chamber and you pull the trigger." Ben aimed the weapon to the ground at his feet. "The piton will go into the rock and hold fast. We'll anchor a rope to it from here and we'll slide down to that ledge just above the cavern."

Standing over his mark in the dust, Ben slipped his finger around the trigger and fired the gun. The piton shot into the ground, burying itself in the rock to its neck, an eye to pass the rope through. Ben stooped over and threaded the black nylon cord through the eye, then fashioned a knot. He pulled the rope taut and yanked on it a few times, testing to make sure it held. Satisfied, he tossed the rope off the ledge while turning to us.

"Same routine, guys. Use your slack to slide down. Make sure you keep your feet under you at all times."

Ben strapped himself to the rope. He had left about five feet between the piton and the edge of the cliff, enough space to safely clamp on. He backed himself over the edge and soon bounded down the side of the wall, bouncing on the balls of his feet, letting the slack carry him down to our desired destination.

"Show-off," I laughed down to him.

"I'm next," Erin reported. Before any of us got the chance to question her sincerity, she clamped herself to the line and backpedaled over the ledge. We watched her slowly work down the side of the wall, taking small, forced plods, shimmying the rope through her hands in small stretches. She set down on the ledge with Ben, and remained as he did, attached to the line by her vest and holding part of the rope in her right hand.

Tanner worked through the final checklist before beginning his descent when he stopped short of the rope. "You feel that?" he murmured.

"No," I said. "Feel what?"

Tanner brushed his thinning hair with his hands. "Hopefully nothing," he quickly spouted. "I felt a tremor."

"How big?" Dad asked.

"Bigger than it should be," Tanner replied as he buckled himself to the line.

DOME OF THE ROCK

"Perfect," Jack lamented. "As if nothing else could go wrong."

"Quit your whining, bitch," Tanner retorted as he disappeared over the side. "It's nothing. I promise."

I watched Tanner as he lowered himself down the slope. His muscles tensed a lot more than necessary to control his body weight. Either he was seriously out of shape or something more was going on. I wiped my brow clean of sweat as Jack scrambled down the eastern wall, from the spot we stood on to a ledge twenty-five feet below.

I prepared to go next when Dad grabbed me by my forearm. "Before we continue, I want to give you something."

"What is it, Dad?"

"Since it's your birthday, it's only right to give you a present."

"You don't need to, Dad. I don't mind. Really."

He shook me off. "No, you truly deserve it. Besides, it's supposed to be a special day for you. Let me do this."

"Fair enough, Dad," I reluctantly agreed, "go ahead. What do you have for me?"

Dad thrust his right hand into his pants pocket. He fished in the dark pocket for a second or two before pulling his fist free. When it came out, a thin rope chain dangled between his fingers.

"This was once your mother's. I bought it for her when we were courting. I know she'd be proud knowing that I'd given it to you."

He presented the object to me, face up in his now open palm. The thin chain connected to a simple circular locket, a nondescript oval of silver metal. Faint scratches crisscrossed the surface. It shone in the noon day sunlight, momentarily blinding me by flashing my retinas.

"Wow," I whispered. I clutched the locket in my right hand. "Thank you."

"Look inside, Pickle," Dad whispered back.

I folded the front of the locket on its hinge, revealing the interior of the piece of jewelry. Inside, I found a black and white photo of a beautiful woman. Her large eyes gleamed back at me, her flowing hair filled the oval, and her round jaw released a perfect smile. The picture was no larger than my thumb.

"That's a picture of your mother," Dad muttered. His voice cracked under the pressure of the sadness.

I stared down at the first photo I'd ever seen of her. "I don't know what to say."

"She looked forward to you," Dad choked out. "When you were born, I vowed to give you this when you became a man. Today, you proved yourself to me."

We both sniffled quietly together. I looked at Dad, he returned the gaze, and, simultaneously, we reached to each other and accepted the other's embrace. Tears streamed from both of us as we held each other for over a minute.

I thought of what he meant to me. I remembered how Dad always made it to all my games, recitals, class projects, and parents' nights. He always found time for us, whether we wanted him there or not. When I couldn't multiply, he took time away from himself to teach me. When Jack wanted to learn to ride his motorcycle, Dad made sure to be there to catch him before he fell over. Some people don't like to express their love for their Dad, especially guys who don't think their fathers are cool enough or young enough or bold enough. Hugging him there, on the top of the mountain, I hoped he understood that I found him to be good enough.

I ended our hug by pulling myself away from him. "Let's go make history, Dad," I said as I put the chain around my neck and fastened the clasp.

"No, son," Dad replied. "Let's go find history."

CHAPTER 24

The six of us met up once more as we huddled together on the narrow ledge that served as a balcony over the cavern we wished to explore. We all had our backs flattened against the rock, staying as far from the edge of the lip as possible. Although the rock wall did not lay truly perpendicular to the surface of the lava dome, we still couldn't see the ground below us from our spot because of the nearly ninety degree angle of the facade.

A gentle breeze licked our faces as we remained stationary on the ledge. Ben had rigged a crude barricade between us and the edge, firing two pitons into the wall and fastening a length of rope between them. We buckled ourselves to the cable, which slackened only slightly between the two posts. Nobody made any movements, for fear of falling over the edge to the sure death below.

"Now what?" Jack queried. "What do we do now?"

"Patience son," Dad replied. "Ben, any ideas."

"Sir, we can get to the cave from here. We'll each lower ourselves over the lip to the next ledge below. It's slightly thicker than this one and should prove no problem for us."

"You want to die here, don't you Dewey?" Jack leaned forward to rip into Ben.

"Close your mouth and do what I say," Ben fired back. Jack carefully lifted his middle finger to Ben.

"God I'm tired of heights," Erin added. She kept her eyelids tightly shut as she clung to the ledge.

I breathed in deeply for a moment while the others constructed the plan. They may have failed to notice, but the view we had was breathtaking. From our high perch, the valley below stretched out in the plushest shade of green. The sunlight intermingled with the metamorphic shards of earth scattered about the northwestern portion of the island. Faint clouds of foam wisped into the air beyond the fragments, a glistening layer of spray lifting on the horizon. I could faintly see our tent village down to the west, only because my tent was blaze orange and set itself apart from the surrounding tan field it rested in. I immersed myself in the pristine scene before me until I was nudged in the ribs by Tanner, immediately to my right.

"It's your turn," he mumbled. "Go."

I shook the cobwebs from my mind and slid carefully to my left. I reached the corner of the ledge, where it disappeared into the wall. A part of the corner sloped down, more gently than the angle of the cliff's surface. Below me, two sets of arms reached up, ready to assist me to the level from which their owners awaited me. I swung first one leg, then the other, over the ledge and pushed myself beyond the point of return.

Dropping to the next flat area, I found myself pulled into a gaping opening in the rock. Erin and Dad waited for me there while Ben and Jack stayed outside the cave's entrance, staring up at Tanner's feet, which dangled down toward them. He dropped to the cavern soon enough as well. Ben removed his sunglasses as the six of us stooped under the short ceiling of this pathway to the interior of the high eastern crag.

"A little tight fit, Seamus," Tanner remarked. He brushed dust from his follicles.

"Dark too," Dad added.

Jack fished a lighter from his pocket. "I'll give us light."

"No!" Tanner protested. He slapped the lighter from Jack's grasp. It bounced out of the cave, teetered on the edge, and disappeared over the side forever.

"What the fuck!" Jack bellowed, clutching at his own wrist.
"You don't know what kind of gases are in here," Tanner explained. "Your lighter might've ignited something. We'd have been fired out of here like six separate rockets. It's best to use the flashlights."

"Um, Tanner," I asked, "um…what flashlights?"

Tanner looked at me like I farted. "Flashlight then," he said, and he illuminated the cavern with the flick of a button on his portable lamp. The round beam cut a swath of light over the dark rock tunnel.

The first thing I noticed was the lack of stalactites and stalagmites. The cave didn't seem to have any kind of protrusions either dropping from the ceiling or rising from the floor. Next, I noted that the moisture content in the cave was minimal at best. There seemed to be little sign of the muggy air often associated with these types of rock formations. In addition, it didn't appear that this cave had been tread in before, not by creatures of our advancement anyway. There were no signs of life visiting the cavern, no discarded tools, no pictographs, no remains of a fire pit. This cave appeared to be virgin soil to the human race, which seemed particularly odd considering what Dad thought might be in here. I figured that, at the very least, there would be some sort of evidence that would help prove that man or god once walked in there.

Finally, I realized that the temperature inside this enclosed space was nearly unbearable.

I stripped off my shirt, reducing my coverage to a white tank top and khaki jeans. Jack and Ben followed my lead, removing a layer of clothing each from their backs. Erin rolled the sleeves of her short sleeved shirt to her shoulders and tied the waist in a knot. Her green bandanna began to darken under the moist sweat pouring from her brow. Even Dad and Tanner lessened the amount of clothes they wore, removing tops and stripping to their underclothes. We piled our discarded belongings near the mouth of the cave.

Tanner stopped in his tracks and raised his index finger to his lips. He held his palm up, serving to stop us from moving. "Against the wall," he muttered in a low voice.

Before we could ask why, the cave grumbled to life. The rock shook violently from side to side. Footing became nearly impossible as the whole cavern rumbled around us, the ground beneath feeling as though it rose and fell in rolling waves. I snatched Erin and held her head tight to me as I pressed her between me and the wall. After more than ten seconds, the shaking ceased.

"Let's get the fuck out of here," Jack pleaded. "No goddamn gate to heaven is worth this shit."

"I agree," Tanner said. "Seamus, I don't like this."

Dad rubbed his right eye under his glasses. Contrary to his usual routine, he rubbed for a long time, seconds upon seconds. He sighed deeply, contemplating his options carefully. I could tell because he pulled his glasses from his face. Whenever he did that, I knew Dad struggled with a personal problem that required his full attention.

Dad bent over to claim the flashlight, dropped by Tanner during the tremor. Dad squatted to his knees and reached for it. As he grasped it, his eyes followed the direction of the beam. He remained in the hunched position, slid his glasses back on his face, and motioned for me to join him.

"What do you think, Pickle?" he muttered, barely audible, even as the words reverberated inside the dark corners of the cavern.

I followed the flashlight's beam to where it impacted the back wall of the cave. "Let's try it, Dad."

Dad rose to his feet and pushed past the rest of the group and to the cave's mouth. He produced his cell phone and punched ten quick digits into it. Tanner began to ask him what he was doing, but Dad cut him off with a simple flat palm toward Tanner's face. Dad pressed the phone to his ear and waited for an answer.

"That's right. No, I need you here soon. Yes, forty-five minutes. Yes, on the plateau." Dad gulped in more air. He drummed his left hand on his pant leg.

"Listen, Mr. Cheney. No, on the plateau. Well, find a way. We die here otherwise. If we're not there yet, wait for us. I'll call you soon. Bye."

"I don't like this," Tanner protested.

"Listen Tanner, listen children. Come here." Dad motioned for us to follow him as he crawled to the far interior wall of the cavern. He kept the flashlight trained on the wall itself. He stopped five feet from the enclosed end of the tunnel and dropped down to a seated position, his legs extended flat in front of him. He handed me the light.

"There's an opening here," he explained. "I'd like to check it out, and Jared would too."

"Ah, fuck this," Tanner cursed. "No, Seamus. No."

Dad pawed at the area of his interest. He rolled small fragmented rock samples from the cut in the enclosed wall. Some of the pieces crumbled to dust when thrown against other chunks of rock.

"I'll make a bargain with you. Give me a half hour to explore this. I've already called for the helicopter. If we don't find anything by the time it should be here, we'll get out of here. After all, what's the likelihood of another quake like what we just had?"

Tanner began to pace in the darkness. "Seamus, it's more than one quake. I've felt them all day. I know I said that the possibility of a catastrophic event while we were here was about as likely as winning the lottery. I forgot to realize that people win the lottery every two weeks."

"Fine. You can wait here if you want." Dad turned to the rest of us. "That goes for each of you too. Anybody who wants to stay here can. Son, if you're ready. Let's go."

Dad flattened himself against the ground, on his stomach, and began inching his way under an opening in the rock. The hole at the end of the tunnel was three feet high and about four feet wide, a small crack of an area to squeeze through. I followed Dad, handing the flashlight to Erin. Ben shimmied through after me, Jack actually joined us, shockingly, and Erin brought the light with her as we crawled along through this narrow shaft on our bellies.

CHAPTER 25

All I heard in my ears was my own heart beating as I bellied my way through the narrow shaft. The tight tunnel continued forward for more than thirty feet before I saw Dad go upright in front of me. The flashlight Erin carried, three people behind me, faintly lit the path. I reached an area where the cramped ceiling lifted, and I stood next to Dad.

"This is interesting," he muttered. He felt along the face of the rock, the same rock we just passed through. His voice echoed hollowly around us in the darkness. Ben emerged from the tunnel, standing and patting dirt from his chest.

"God," Ben beamed, "this is more fun by the minute."

Jack broke free from the cramped quarters and joined us in our upright stance. Light began to pour out of the tube, and within seconds, Erin pulled herself free and into the new cavern we now occupied. She handed Dad the flashlight as she removed dust from her hair as best she could, shaking her head like a wet Springer spaniel after a dip in the lake.

"Wow children. Take a look at this." Dad directed the beam from the flashlight around the new cave. He started with the high ceiling, probably more than twelve feet from the floor. The walls were more rounded than the outer cave, and the interior chamber we now stood in felt a lot moister. In fact, in the pale light, I saw that Dad's glasses now fogged with condensation. This immense cavern easily dwarfed the other, being at least four times the size of the first hole in the rock. Dad slowly moved the light along the ceiling and down the far enclosed space.

"Oh my God," he slowly shuddered. He stood stationary, with the flashlight's beam trained on the floor of the cave.

The light glinted off a shimmering surface, a sheet that covered two-thirds of the cavern's floor. The sheet shone silver in the light, quite possibly the first light to ever meet this mass. The surface stayed quiet, not showing any type of movement within itself. Dad handed Ben the flashlight and stepped forward, to the edge.

"The Urdar fountain," he pronounced under a hushed breath.

"What, Dad?"

"I…think this…kids, this might…might be the Urdar fountain." Dad plunged his hands into the pool of water and splashed a scoop of the contents over his face. Ripples ringed out over the surface, moving out from where he broke the plane and toward the far reaches of the pool.

"It's not hot, kids. It's tepid like the faucet back home." He swallowed a fistful of the clear liquid. The grin on his face could cover two city blocks.

"The Urdar fountain was the fountain of knowledge," Dad explained to us from his knees. "It's where Odin went when he needed advice or comfort. He'd wander under the shadow of the tree of life and consult with the fountain of knowledge."

"You think this is it?" Jack asked. His disbelief bounced off the cave walls.

"I think it might be, son."

"You don't sound smarter if you belief that shit."

Dad frowned, a look that was intensified under the shadows. "Haven't you ever believed in anything you couldn't prove, son?"

"Not really," Jack replied. "Okay, if this is that fountain of knowledge, then where's your tree of life? Huh?"

I heard Dad muttering that it must be there under his breath. He sat with his weight on the back of his lower legs, his upper body rigid and upright. He remained on the shore of the clear pool, flashing his eyes back and forth throughout the grotto.

"Ben, move the light around a little, please."

Ben slowly scanned the cavern with the lamp, moving from the left, over Dad, and to the right. As the flashlight's emission of light touched the right edge of the cavern, Dad ordered him to stop.

The beam of light landed on a large slab of what looked to be shale. It had smooth round edges with grooves in them. This rock was toppled on one side, resting at a forty-five degree angle against the side of the cavern wall. A smaller piece of rock lay under the closest end to us. It appeared as though the larger boulder had broken from its junior counterpart.

Dad reached out and ran his palm over the boulder's surface. This piece was larger around than Dad was tall and took up the right quarter of the cavern. Dad stroked the boulder gently with his fingertips, then wrapped himself over it and embraced the gray slab.

"Does this count?" he asked, his trembling voice repeating throughout the dark earth room.

We all stood behind him, dumbfounded. This large slab of mineral deposit looked very much like a toppled tree trunk, the smaller portion peculiarly close in shape to a dead stump.

"And the dragon Nidhug chewed through the root of the tree of life. The tree trembled from its tallest bough. Then, the tree of life fell."

Dad turned to us. "The gate's here. It's in here."

We fanned out in the cavern, pawing through the faint light. I felt my way along the left side of the grotto, looking high and low for another passage. I worked my way around the shore of the pool until I reached a point where the dry land ended and the water took over.

Ben handed Erin the flashlight and waded into the pool. He walked across the shallow pond, which never grew deeper than a foot to the bottom. He pushed through the water to the far wall and started feeling along the wall the same way I did. Ben covered the portion of the cave that could only be reached in the water, the part of the cavern floor under the surface of the quiet pool.

Dad climbed over the tree shaped rock and hopped to the far side of the large boulder. He felt along the right side of the cave like Ben and I did in the other parts of the cavern. He stopped when he reached the shore of the pool, a spot in a far corner of the naturally formed chamber.

"Screw this," Jack commented to Erin. He lowered himself to the tunnel entrance and squeezed himself into the opening.

"Come back!" Erin pleaded. "Jared! Jack's leaving!" Her words hit my ears three separate times.

I waved at her. "Let him go," I said, "so he can be ready to go." He wasn't providing much assistance with his complaining.

I reached an area in the rock where I felt a shelf in the wall. I slid my hands around the area carefully, hoping that maybe it opened up, either above or below the shelf. All I found was more solid rock.

"Anything Dewey?" I called out to Ben. In the shadows, I saw his head nod negatively.

"You Dad?" I said. My words bounced back to me.

"No, son," he said softly and slowly. "No. Nothing here."

I thought I heard his heart snap in two, the sound echoing in a hushed tone off the smoothed edges of the chamber.

A small rectangle of green light rose from a position near the far edge of the pond. I caught a glimpse of Dad in the pale green glow, his head lowered and looking directly into what proved to be the internal lamp of his cell phone.

"It's a half hour, kids." His words sounded forced as they trickled from his lips. "I guess it's time we left."

The light went out and I heard a slow splashing in the pool. Two separate dark forms pushed their way in the low light, heading toward the glow from the flashlight. The light flashed on to me directly as I heard Erin's rushed words circle around me.

"Look at the pond."

DOME OF THE ROCK

For a second, I, like Ben and Dad, froze in place. Erin directed the flashlight beam on the surface of the water. A series of bubbles began to burst forth on the formerly calm surface. Ripples started to spread out from somewhere near the center of the pool, nowhere near Dad or Ben, who were both almost to Erin on the shore when they stopped. I placed my right hand on the wall next to me, acting on a hunch I hoped was untrue.

As I touched the smooth surface, created from centuries of activity, a crack appeared under my hand. The cave began to hiss in the darkness, and the water rumbled to life, like the low setting of a Jacuzzi. Erin dropped the flashlight into the pond, and as it floated down, the prismatic refracted light dimly illuminated the entire cave. Fissures were forming in what should be solid rock. A loose chunk smashed into the pond, which sprayed the suddenly warmer water into my hair.

"Ah, figs," Dad snarled.

We had awakened the island, and the island was grumpy.

CHAPTER 26

The sound of hissing steam rose in my ears as I bounded through the pond. The water around my ankles bubbled wildly and pieces of rock the size of marbles fell from the ceiling and rolled from the walls. The temperature inside the room began to increase and faint crackles snapped from everywhere.

"Go!" I yelled. "I'm right behind you!"

All I could see in the pale glow of the flashlight, now resting on the bottom of the pool, was the tan soles of Ben and Dad's boots as they ducked into the tunnel under the rock. Erin waited for me at the entrance, almost frozen.

"We gotta go Erin!" I screamed.

"It's going to fall on us!" she screeched back. She refused to move, her eyes each the size of the radio telescopic dish in Puerto Rico. Her whites drew me to the correct spot.

"Better to be crushed than baked," I replied as I pushed her toward the hole. She resisted my first effort then backpedaled from my shove before spinning and dropping to the floor. She quickly shimmied into the tunnel like a rabbit, pumping her limbs in the dust for all she was worth. I let her disappear before dropping down. As I did so, I caught one last glance of the Earth itself falling in around me.

The second I ducked in the hole, I heard a thunderous crash behind me. As the loud sound shot out, a gust of heated wind overtook me from behind, and the tunnel went pitch black. The cramped tunnel snatched the breath from me, and I coughed in powdery dirt as I furiously crawled on my belly toward the opening I knew existed just ahead.

The ground under me shook in waves. I continued pawing my way along in the darkness, keeping my body moving forward, refusing to hesitate to find out what was happening around me. All I knew was that the ground under me swayed, the rock above me crackled, and my heart pumped at such a rate that I thought it might jump from my body like the transmission from a 1972 Dodge Charger. My scared limbs flailed frantically through the small tunnel, and I could feel superficial cuts opening on my palms, my elbows, and my kneecaps.

I moved as fast as I could, but I never caught Erin in the tunnel. I thought I was going to overrun her for sure with the velocity I carried through the hollow tube. Her safety mattered as much as my own at that point, and I was relieved to find that she ignored her extreme fear at the most critical moment and let her athletic body do the work her frightened psyche couldn't direct. She would most certainly die, and probably take me with her, if she let her mind take over. I slipped as I thought of her, and my left eyebrow was sliced open by the gravel as I momentarily went face down in the floor.

The mountain let out a loud wailing cry around me and my heart pounded still harder. I felt a surge of energy come over me as the creaking noise filled my ears and echoed in my bones. I pushed my body even harder than before. It responded with strength that welled up from the spot in one's body where the fear of death lies. It came from the spot where one pulls the strength to live, to hold their breath underwater for thirty more seconds, to refuse to lie down in the face of danger, to box Death's ears before he gets his chance at you. There was no medical term for this body part, I just knew it existed, a knowledge that came to me after it kicked in and made me rush through the tunnel with the speed and sure footing of a squirrel.

I was bathed in pure black as I pressed on. Then, from nowhere, a hand jumped into the hole and snatched me at my collar. The appendage pulled me from the hole as I made the effort to climb from what would have been my tomb in moments had I not moved so fast. The light, although pale, was surely more welcome to me than the pitch blackness I emerged from.

"Thanks," I said to Ben as I rolled to my feet.

Ben helped me from the ground as Dad and Erin looked over Jack. Jack was sprawled on his back on the floor of the cavern, his Red Sox hat knocked from his scalp. A trickle of fresh blood escaped a cut on his forehead and he struggled to accept the extended arms Dad and Erin presented to him. His face curled in a pained grimace.

"He just flipped out and ran," Jack spurted. He dabbed at the blood running outside his left eye with his fingers. I noticed that, as he spewed forth the explanation, Tanner was missing.

"He threw me to the ground when I told him to wait for you. He said this place was going to blow and he wasn't dying with the rest of us. Then he knocked me senseless. That skinny shit sure packs some strength."

"Where'd he go?" Dad asked.

"Out the cave."

"I suggest we follow his lead."

We rushed to the open entrance of the cave in unison. Our ten feet stepped as one, doing little more than floating across the bedrock as we hurried toward the bright light. I slid to a halt as I reached the mouth of the cavern, pushing small bits of gravel over the lip and to the valley below. The cave continued to growl in the dark. I heard another creaking noise.

The rush of air and noise from the collapsing far interior wall of the exterior cavern nearly collapsed my eardrums. It almost sounded like a car wreck, the snapping of plastic, the shrill cries of steel to pavement, the unmistakable high pitched squeal of impending death. I shielded my face from the rushing gust, a concussive blast that attempted to push me off the ledge and down the hillside. I fought the wave that crashed over me, ducking into the force that hit me. My four companions did the same, letting the blast overtake them but not steal their choice to live.

"Everyone all right?" I called out. I was met with four positive nods.

We stood in the mouth of the cavern, a group of five, when we noticed a series of pebbles clapping down the side of the ledge from above. We heard a shriek and instantly ducked into the open sky on the ledge. We looked up to find Tanner, his tall build working up the black nylon cord, straining to reach the flat plateau on the roof of the now active volcano.

"Hold on a minute! Tanner!" Dad yelled.

Tanner ignored us, flashing a glance and resuming his frantic climb in the matter of a blink. He scaled the cable with a hand over hand motion, his legs providing little help to his cause. The footing on the nearly vertical embankment lacked existence; there weren't any holds to force one's toe into, to provide some sort of support for the task. His face contorted in terror as he fought the mountainside, his feet sliding from beneath him as he strained to reach further height, in his mind more of a chance at life.

"He's not buckled on the line," Ben reported as he stared up through the sunglasses he placed back across his nose's bridge.

Tanner's feet stutter stepped on the facade, the result of him trying to find any foothold. Gravity pulled at him as he tried to fight the force. His hands tightened on the lifeline, and his face flushed crimson as he used every bit of strength within him to attempt to climb to the sky.

Ben spoke again. "He's not going to make it."

Dad rushed his voice up the crag. "Tanner! Come down! The helicopter's on its way!"

"I've got to go!" Tanner screamed back without removing his eyes from the wall in front of him. He strained up once more, forcing his right hand higher on the line.

As he made his move, the ridge moaned under the weight of the pressure building within it. It seemed to reduce in size for a second then the energy burst forth from within once more. I covered my head and hid under the lip above me, knowing that what little cover it provided beat being in the open. The rest of my group followed my lead.

Then I heard what would best be described as the sound a shot deer made the instant before life exited through its eyes. The sound was a sharp cry, a bawl of sadness coupled with the sheer terror of knowing nothing could delay the end. It was the type of sickening noise that kept me from the meadow and rifle my entire life. I detested the thought of making another living creature subject to the events that brought that sound bubbling to the surface. The silence would come first, then the pop. Seconds later, that cry would ring out, and soon after, the great unknown beyond beckoned. I hated that sound.

The sickening terror shout came from up the side of the ridge. More rock fell as the five of us stumbled to the mouth of the cave again. We looked up to see Tanner once more.

His screaming had ceased as he dangled from the nylon cable, gripping the thin black cord with only his left hand. His feet kicked at the wall wildly, twin pistons hoping to find any way to rescue the rest of their master. In his shock, his right arm failed to do much more than claw at the rock face, finding nothing to gain a grip on. He struggled as his left hand slowly loosened and he started sliding a couple inches.

Then, without him even seeing it, a larger boulder, about the size and shape of a television set, toppled from above, cut loose from the wall itself. The rock crashed down and collided with Tanner. He stood no chance.

He was probably lucky in a way. I was certain a rock of that girth slamming unimpeded into one's skull would pretty much kill anybody. The rock bounced him from the rope and pulled him down the side of the ridge. It crashed along down to the valley floor, where the steam had grown thicker and more visually intense. Tanner crashed off the lip above the cave we waited in, bounded over the ledge in front of us, and bounced a couple more times off the side of the hill before finding his final resting place at the bottom of the wall. Each of us screamed for him. A knot tied itself in my stomach.

Dad crossed himself as he leaned out of the cave. "My friend, you will be sorely missed." He paused for a moment then looked to the sky. "My lord, please make that the only one of us you take today. We all still have work to do for you here."

A couple clouds passed overhead. The wind stopped howling into the cave. As we stepped out onto the ledge, the mountain growled across the valley below.

CHAPTER 27

"What do we do now?" I asked. I didn't care who answered, I just hoped somebody had an idea. Anything would work.

"Die," Jack replied. Anything but that would do.

"Not on my watch," Ben retorted. He grabbed the cable that we'd left between the two pitons on the ledge above. He pulled himself up, kicking his legs to his right simultaneously. His feet scratched their way on top of the ledge, and he rolled himself to the safety of the surface. He leaned over the edge, offering his healthy left hand to us.

"Come on," he ordered.

Erin happily accepted his proposal first. She wrapped her right hand around his left wrist and he strained to pull her up. We helped him by boosting her from below. The process repeated itself with Jack and Dad, no problems as they climbed to the ledge above, a safer point as long as more Sony sized boulders didn't pick us clean from the surface of the world. Jack took over for Ben and offered his hand to me. I grabbed it with my right hand and tightened my left around the nylon cable.

As I relinquished contact with the ledge below by pushing off, the hillside popped. The was no other way to describe it. The island literally up and popped. The sound, the force of the blast, the shudder the ridge felt, it burst. I wrapped my left elbow over the cable as Jack lost hold of me. Luckily, and amazingly, he was thrown back toward the wall instead of over the side.

"Shit!" I screamed as I kicked my feet at the lip of the upper ledge.

I hung by one arm, which was being pinched inside the elbow by the cruel rope. Heat rose from my skin as the rope branded it. I refused to let go and threw my right hand out at it. I caught a grip on it and forced my right foot onto the ledge. Jack snatched me by my collar and pulled with all his might, dragging me to safety.

"Thanks bro," I forced out through my lack of breath.

"Not now," he replied. "We're nowhere yet."

"What the hell was that?" I wondered aloud. I rubbed at the interior fold of my elbow, a stretch of flesh scarred with a stripe of deep red.

"The dome exploded," Dad calmly reported. He pointed over my shoulder and to the area just below us, where the simple cavern once stood.

In its place, a gaping scar ran diagonally up to the left, starting below and right of the cave and ending a good twenty feet away from and ten feet above us. Boulders slipped from the crevice, or, more accurately, they launched from the crack in groups. These things were being thrown to the valley below, in pieces ranging in size from gravel to Volkswagen Beetle. As more rock fell forth, I noticed that some pieces were glowing hot, a pale orange at first and then, as more rocks started raining out, a deeper red color. The ridge spit them forth like watermelon seeds.

"Where the hell's Whirlygirl?" Ben yelled to Dad.

"On it," Dad replied, fumbling over the keypad on his cell phone.

"Where are you?" Dad screamed into the phone. Over the rumbling noise, I couldn't tell if an answer even came.

Dad clicked the phone off. "He says he's on top of us." He looked down at the personal cellular system in his palm.

"We won't need this again," he said, and flipped it underhand into the sunlit abyss.

Seconds later, a different sound entered my ears. It remained faint, but it could have been within my head at that point and still have been muffled. The sheer violence of the volcano we cowered on drowned out any other possible noises. Still, that faint noise, the faint sound of hope, grew slightly louder. That noise of life, the steady whirring, continued to present itself, a little clearer with each second. Then, hope took the form of reality.

The shadow of what resembled a dragonfly swept over us in an instant, and the sexiest woman I'd ever seen, Whirlygirl, turned a sharp left in front of our position. She slowed to a hover near the same altitude as us and held fast. Mullet Joe peeked through the side of the windscreen, having aerially parked the aircraft with its passenger side presented to us. The sliding door into the fuselage lay open.

"Now what do we do?" I asked in a rushed voice.

Jack took a step to the ledge and motioned for Mullet Joe to come closer.

He looked over his shoulder to us. "I've got this."

CHAPTER 28

Mullet Joe piloted Whirlygirl high over us until the helicopter hovered directly above us. Jack directed traffic from our position with a series of gestures, telling Mullet Joe to move closer, up, and over us. With Mullet Joe in place, Jack flashed another signal, spinning his hands like a traveling call in basketball, running each fist over and under the other. Mullet Joe nodded and flipped a button on his console.

The cord attached to the winch hummed from its spool, cascading down toward us from the heavens. Jack watched the line drop and caught the end as it reached him. He held it in his left hand and tied the free end around his waist.

"Okay Dewey, it's on you now," Jack said over the rumbling of the mountain and the whirring of the rotor blades. "You know what's needed."

"You bet your sweet ass," Ben replied.

"Not today."

Jack signaled Mullet Joe by flashing a thumbs up to him. Joe pulled his head back inside the cockpit from the open pilot's window and flipped the toggle switch again. Jack slowly rose in the sky on the lifeline, pulling closer to the craft and the relatively safe interior of the flying rust bucket of a war bird.

Jack dangled about ten feet below the deck of Whirlygirl when the winch began to jolt him on the cord. It coughed once, hacked a second time, then died. Jack hung from beneath the aircraft, drifting slowly in a twisting circle. Mullet Joe flipped the switch a few times, then ducked his head out the window and shrugged. Jack saw the gesture and flashed one of his own, making sure to do so fast and with only one hand, keeping the other tightly wrapped in the rope.

Jack started working his way up the line, hand over hand, inching closer to the belly of the Huey. I couldn't hear him over the two prevalent noises of the helicopter and the rumbling ridge, but if watching football all my life taught me anything, it was how to read lips, especially profanity screamed from a head coach on the sidelines. Jack's mouth spit what looked to be the equivalent of what poured forth when one of those European soccer style placekickers shanked an extra point off the crossbar. Every move he made was matched by a series of open throated bellows, inaudible to us below him.

Jack reached the landing runner of the Huey and slung his legs over it. He carefully transferred his weight to the skid and quickly uncoiled the rope from the winch. He found the end of the line, the span between him and it floating in space below him. He quickly cut the rope from the spool with a knife in his left hand while he clung to the skid with his right.

"This complicates things," I stated. My words were met with the crashing of rock around us, as a cloud of steam started to rise from the deep scar in the cliff's face.

Jack let the end of rope fall from his grip, which caused no problem since he knew the important part of the rope was anchored around his waist. He threw himself into the fuselage, rolling forward from the skid before rising to his feet. He looked down to us and flashed a signal to Ben.

Ben turned to face the wall and raised his piton gun. He pulled the trigger and the pin shot forth into the rock. Buried to its neck, the piton rang out a clanking noise as it embedded itself. Ben flailed at the rope, which dangled on the edge of his grasp.

Jack undid the rope from his waist and took the end to a metal rod tucked just under the ceiling inside the sliding door. He flipped the link over the pole, tied it in a square knot, leaned against the rope with his weight, flipped another link over the top, and tied a second knot to the first. He hung on the rope, pulling the cable flush against the metal pole. I could see the pressure he put on the cable from where I stood, on the ledge below with my back pressed against the hillside.

Meanwhile, Ben repeated the process around the piton. He slipped the cord through the pinhead, wrenched it into a knot, pulled it taut, and tied it once more to make sure. He waved to Jack, who returned the wave and jumped to the cockpit.

Whirlygirl slowly slipped from directly above us and into the path of the afternoon sun. A plume of filthy steam rose toward her from the island's surface, but it broke under the force of her whirring blades. She lowered to a level just below us, no more than five feet lower than us and about fifteen feet from the rock. Her whining blades blew hot air into our faces, a surprising sensation given the amount of heat in the air already.

"Do precisely what I do," Ben ordered. He removed his climbing vest from the cable, a move the remaining three of us copied.

Ben strapped the attached clamp to the line, the vest sagging down on either side of the fastener. He wrapped his arm into the open hole, winding the material around his elbow counterclockwise before tightening his grip over the straps. He performed the process with first his left side and then his right.

"Will this work?" I asked him. My eyes were huge and glassy, my hair filling with ash.

"Did Dwight Evans hit the first pitch of the 1986 season for a home run?"

I paused for a moment, trying to think whether that was true of not. "I sure hope he did," I shrugged, patting Ben on the back.

Ben picked his feet up from the ground and started sliding down the line on his clamp. The line sagged between the cliff and the helicopter, above the gaping opening of the cavern and below the hastily spinning rotor. Ben hummed along the nylon cable, quickly passing over the grand abyss below and to the helicopter. His clamp met the side of the metal rod inside the aircraft, and the force tugged his damaged right wrist from its grip. He crashed in a heap inside the craft, slamming the damaged wrist into the interior wall of the Huey. He winced on the floor, but he was much better off than the rest of us.

Jack gestured for another of us to cross the lifeline. I volunteered Erin to go next, and she stepped to the edge of the lip.

"You going to be okay?" I asked. I held her vest in place until she secured herself within the tangle of straps.

"Yeah," she responded, "I think I'll be fine."

"You're not worried about the height?"

She looked down for a heartbeat. "Fuck that," she groaned. "I'd rather fall than burn."

Dad gave her a quick hug before I pecked her on her twin beautiful lips. "I'll be right there," I whispered as I gently nudged her from the ledge.

Erin slid comfortably across the nylon line, bouncing a couple times but otherwise enjoying a smooth ride. She arrived at the open side of the helicopter, where both Ben and Jack waited for her. They made sure she arrived safely, catching her as she reached them and pulling her into the craft. She unwound herself from the climbing apparatus and grabbed a seat within the sanctity of Whirlygirl, twisting her face away from Jack when he attempted to give her a kiss of his own.

"You're next, Dad," I reported.

"No, Pickle," he replied. "I want you to go."

DOME OF THE ROCK

As he spoke, a feeling of dread climbed into me. My father rarely talked in a voice other than the lecturing style he was accustomed to. When he did, the change couldn't be ignored. His voice lost sharpness when he succumbed to emotion, especially disappointment or sadness. The change was obvious, especially since I knew the resulting inflections and tone from experience. As he rolled that sentence through a thickening New England drawl, I chose to nip the problem in the bud.

"I insist, Dad," I argued.

"No, son," Dad lamented.

"Just go," I insisted. "Don't worry about me. We'll meet up on the other end. I promise."

Jack waved to us, trying to draw one of us to the line by frantically gesturing for one of us to get going. I hugged my father close before lifting his vest to the cable and tightening the clamp over the line. Dad reluctantly bound himself within the vest, wearily pushing each arm among the straps and creating a secure grip on the garment. He pushed himself from the ledge, and as he skidded across the line, I gave him his own salute. I cocked my head right, pressed my index and middle finger to my eyebrow, extended it to him, and pulled the hand back to my brow once more. Dad reached the far side of the rope, allowing Jack and Ben to pull him to the interior of the aircraft. I watched Dad duck into the cockpit and I readied myself for my own crossing.

Pebbles continued to rain down around me. Then, another pop emerged from within the crag, muffled but still a distressing noise to hear. Steam poured from both the valley floor and the hole in the wall, a thicker, darker smoke of a rising steam. The gray smog grated at my eyes as it rose over me. The helicopter shuddered against the blast, and the lifeline skipped in the air.

"We are the Black Bears from the shores of the Brandh, filled with nobility," I choked in the ash. I grasped the clasp in my fist.

"Always with pride through the countryside, we walk with a glide, strive to survive." I slapped the clamp over the line and secured the metal binder fast around the rope.

"So when you come up against one of our den," I coughed forth through the rising cloud. My hands wound themselves around the fabric of the vest in simultaneous circles. I gulped in dirty air and hacked on a mess of microscopic particles.

"Know that it's best to flee." Truer words were never spoken. The ridge rumbled once again. This time, a spout of hot rock spewed from the crack just below me. Magma spurt forth into the sunlit sky, glowing liquid that splashed into the basin below.

I waited a moment for the lava pouring forth to subside just a tiny bit. When it calmed to what I considered a safe enough level, I counted to three in my head and threw myself forward over the ledge.

"Cause we'll Fight!" I hummed along the nylon rope, my legs pulled close to my chest at the knees.

"Claw!" I slid under the rotor blades. The rush of wind above me never felt so right.

"Scratch! To the top!" My legs entered the interior of the fuselage first, followed closely by the rest of me. Jack and Ben snatched me close, refusing to let me slip from their firm grasp.

"To vic…tor…y!" I yelled as I unrolled my limbs from the climbing harness and fell to the floor of the aircraft. I lowered my lips to the metal platform and kissed the solid steel that held me in the sky.

Ben sliced the rope with a hunting knife, the titanium blade cutting through interwoven strands with relative ease. The line snapped free and fell from the belly of Whirlygirl, snaking below us on the cross current as it dropped to the hot rock below. I remained on all fours, resting my suddenly tired body, inhaling full loads of oxygen and releasing carbon dioxide in a series of forced deep breaths. I refused to lift myself from my face down position, letting myself collapse against the textured steel of Whirlygirl's interior.

DOME OF THE ROCK

"Get us from here, Mr. Cheney," Dad ordered. Ben thrust the door shut as the helicopter banked to the left, lifting higher into the air over the ravaged island below. I lifted myself from my collapsed position, pulling myself to a seated spot on the bench seat. I shut my eyes for just a moment, listening to the crackling noises around me, the heavy breathing, the hum of the flapping blades.

I rubbed my left thumb and index finger in my tear ducts and opened my eyes as I tried to relieve tension with a squinting motion against my own digits. My exhausted eyelids reluctantly fluttered apart, and I surveyed the scene below me, peering through the window next to my head. I gasped at the scene that awaited me.

Below me, the island struggled with life. The gaping hole in its facade coughed forth molten rock in spurts, spitting loads of magma into the surrounding crater. A few small brush fires raged on the crater floor. A cloud of thin gray ash rose from the gaping wound, billowing miles into the sky in a narrow chimney of smoke. A thinner, clearer white steam also sprang forth from the volcano, emanating from the crater floor. This clearer cloud followed closely along the interior of the crag, rising along the bluff. It parted into two separate forks as it reached the top, as it encountered the haunting Serpent Rock, the only part of the eastern crag still left alone. The only part of the world still left unchanged. Serpent Rock, the only remaining bit of sanity in this hell, stared back at me as I craned my neck to watch it. Of all things, the snake was the only thing that stayed stable.

I cursed that rock to the heavens as the helicopter leveled out and motored away from Baffert Island, from the Dome of the Rock, from the end of my youth, and into the still brilliant New England horizon. It truly was the longest day of the year, if not of all time.

CHAPTER 29

The whole story seems like it happened only yesterday. Every word, every event, every sound, face and place still echoes loudly inside my head. Many people talk of a moment in their lives that shaped the way they lived, a chance encounter or traumatic event that made them the person they are. I can honestly say that my life's path emerged from that weekend.

Everything changed for all of us when Dad got us off that volcano. The first sign came on the helicopter. Jack attempted to console Erin by putting his arm around her. Instead of accepting his effort, Erin shrugged his arm away and looked at him with a contempt in her eye that can only be described as the devil's fire. I looked at Ben and we both agreed, without words exchanged, that those two were through. Our shared thoughts ended up correct as the two of them split almost as soon as we landed at the airfield.

Dad worried me as he sat in the front of the craft with Mullet Joe. Dad made no sounds for the entire flight. He just sat there, looking down his nose through his glasses, watching the land expand in front of us and the sea disappear behind. The only hints of him even being with us on this planet came whenever he would push his fingers under his frames to rub at his right eye. I could see that his brain kept him busy at the time, trying to comprehend how all his efforts to find Ragnarok could go unfulfilled, that Dr. Seamus McCracken returned from his defining journey without reward. For the first time in my life, I sensed vulnerability in my father.

DOME OF THE ROCK

The entire group stayed quiet as we landed at Stanton Airfield. Dad broke his silence with one sentence, muttering lowly, "Please load the car kids." His shoulders slumped and he walked with a step that showed great pain to the van. Each of us helped load up the rig, with the exception of Jack, who chose to smoke a cigarette on the side of the shed. Dad looked at him, shook his head, and rubbed his eye as he struggled into the van.

I knew that a lot of one word responses would follow in the coming weeks.

CHAPTER 30

The silence that owned the group that day continued as each participant reached the curb in front of their respective houses. Ben escaped the anxiety first, receiving his release when the Windstar stopped outside his parents' townhouse. I helped him remove his bags from the cargo space in the back of the van.

"Thanks for coming along, Dewey," I said to him.

"Thanks for having me along," he replied, draping his olive green backpack over his right shoulder and grabbing his empty duffel bag with his left hand. We exchanged a quick fist pound, tapping our knuckles together lightly in friendship. We made sure to do so with our left hands; Ben kept his injured right wrist tucked closely to his body.

"I'll call you," I promised as I climbed into the van. He waved back at me as the cargo door slid shut.

It turned out that Ben's right wrist was not broken. He suffered a severe sprain and mild tendon damage. The damage to his psyche, however, was a little more complicated, as Ben missed the entire summer while resting his wrist. He couldn't climb with his wrist injured like it had been, and he ended up hiking his last summer of freedom away. We talked on a couple of occasions, but Ben's heartbreak at losing all that time kept us from getting together like we wanted. He just lacked the energy that was his trademark.

Ben went on to Boston that fall. He enrolled at Swenson College, graduating in just under five full years with a degree in mathematics. We kept in touch as best two friends can considering the distance, e-mailing whenever the thought crossed our minds and seeing each other whenever time permitted on weekends home.

After college, Ben moved overseas to somewhere in Spain, northwest of Barcelona. He left to teach math in American institutions abroad while at the same time finding himself among the climber friendly Pyrenees Mountains. I'd heard different rumors of him from time to time, one that he returned to Maine, another that he died when he fell into a crevasse. I never confirmed either of these stories, and he didn't make it to our reunion.

I haven't heard from Ben in quite a long time. Sometimes that happens, you lose your best friend to better interests. People grow apart, find themselves with different aspirations in life. Sometimes friendship fades away.

I hope he found what he wanted in life. Maybe someday I'll get to find out.

CHAPTER 31

The next stop was Erin's house. Jack refused to move for her, so she stumbled over him before getting out of the van. She pulled her hair back and secured it in a rubber band as I unloaded her garment bag from the back.

"I'm sorry," I told her. I couldn't think of anything else to say to her at that point.

"Don't be," she replied. With that, she approached me and hugged me deeply. I placed my left hand on the back of her head, holding her close for a minute or so. I looked into the window of the van and saw Jack staring back at me. His eyes pierced my soul, calling for my shame. I blinked back, shooing them away. I had finished apologizing for him after all the years. She turned and scampered up the steps of the porch, never looking back as she reached the door. I watched her go and witnessed the door shut before I rejoined the remaining adventurers.

That summer may have been the longest period of time I ever experienced. Every day seemed like the hottest on record, followed by the next day making the last feel like a breezy autumn day. I worked indoors throughout, serving as transport of foodstuffs for the homeless shelter in Bangor. I also helped Dad transfer some of his files onto computer disk so he could find them easier. I'm not sure why because Dad's computer still sits in the study waiting to be used. Dad kept his written files around and conferred with them whenever he needed. His records still dominate the landscape of his office. The computer still carries a slipcover over it.

The final straw between Dad and Jack came about three weeks after our trip. The whole fight started when Jack came home drunk on a Tuesday morning. Dad knew Jack was drunk, since it was a day of the week that ended in the letter Y.

"Where were you son?" Dad asked.

"Nowhere you need to know," Jack fired back. Jack brought his full artillery, that was for sure. He wanted a fight.

"Yes I do," Dad replied. "I'm your father and I need to know what you are doing and where you are, as long as you're in my house."

"Shut the fuck up, Seamus. You're not my father." Jack stepped toward Dad. "I'm not your son. You dumped Mom, remember?"

"I'm sorry. It was more complicated than that."

"No it wasn't. You're a worthless Dad and were a lousy husband. You ruined both our lives, you coward."

I refused to hear any more. "You better take that back, Jack."

"Or what? What can you do?"

Let's just say I tried my best to do something. I caught him with a right to his jaw before he even thought it might be coming. Jack staggered back against the dining room wall, knocking a plate off the table. The plate shattered on the hardwood floor as I prepared to strike again.

Before I threw my next punch, Dad grabbed me around the waist. "That's enough!" he pleaded, pulling me back from Jack.

Jack looked at me, dumbfounded. He pushed his left hand to his jaw to inspect the damage. I knew I had stung him good with that shot, a shot I had wanted to give him for about twelve years.

"So that's how it is. Fine." Jack tried to get to his feet, not an easy task for him considering how much alcohol flowed through his system. It probably didn't help his cause that I had absolutely flattened him with one shot.

"Fine." Dad turned and left the dining room, plodding up the stairs and to his study.

Jack stomped out of the house after he found his feet in a flurry of short, quick steps and a slamming door. His belongings were waiting for him on the curb when he returned later that day. I made sure of that. No argument commenced, not even a weak protest. Jack collected his belongings into Steven Collins' El Camino and moved away.

Jack's story got worse from there. He kicked around from job to job for a time, working in the mill in Bucksport, the docks in Portland, and a repair shop in Charleton. Five years of Jack's life disappeared in the bottom of a bottle and a series of mistakes, layoffs, and restarts.

After kicking around for awhile, Jack pulled himself from the gutter and began to try to grow up. Shortly after calling me one night, Jack decided to quit drinking. He struggled with it but beat back his demons. He found a steady job working security at Winter Wind Court, a high-rise complex featuring housing for those who could afford the luxury of a tower condominium. He discovered something he excelled at in the job, earning praise from his employers as he gained experience and expertise. Jack applied his skills for a good cause for once, using his high intelligence instead of letting it fall by the wayside. Finding himself a productive member of society fit Jack well. He even found a way to reconnect with Dad, which pleased me more than anything else Jack ever accomplished.

Two years ago this November fifteenth Jack celebrated the end of another successful week at a bar called the Wayfarer in Bushwood, outside of Orono on the expressway. He went there with our friend Mark Bentley, one person Jack had kept in touch with when he dried out. Mark and Jack liked to go out, but Jack no longer fought his drinking problem so he often served as driver for the duo while Mark let off steam. On this evening, Mark celebrated his paycheck especially hard.

Anyway, the two of them sat at the bar, playing the field and shooting the breeze, when this trucker came in from the first snow of the season and sat in the Wayfarer. This guy stood at least six foot three and weighed close to three hundred pounds. The trucker shook his coat off on Mark as he grabbed a worn stool next to him.

"Excuse you," Mark snarled at the behemoth.

"Fuck you, you punk ass," the trucker snorted back.

"What'd you call me, you ..." Mark replied, rising to his feet. However, Jack cut him off in mid sentence by grabbing him and spinning him away from the situation. The trucker snorted a laugh at Mark and turned his attention back to his beer.

The next move was classic Mark and Jack, although Jack didn't take any part in it for once. Jack paid the tab and the two of them walked out into the slowly falling snow. Jack fished in his pockets for the keys to his F-150 pickup truck as Mark peered around in the parking lot. His eyes stopped on a Peterbilt semi-truck parked diagonally across about six spaces, off by itself toward the back corner of the lot.

"It's Golden Car Wash time," Mark stammered, his tongue fighting through the liquor to build the words. He stumbled toward the big rig while Jack pleaded with him to think twice about what he planned.

Simply put, The Golden Car Wash was a trick employed by many college frat boys and other testosterone laden gladiators who needed better things to do with their time. Since beer came in liquid form, every person who drank their fair share needed to expunge the water from their system in some way. This created the golden portion of the program.

The heavy trucker lifted his eyes from his glass and looked out the window to spot Mark standing next to his rig. He rose to his feet as he noticed the position Mark had taken next to the vehicle. He dropped a ten dollar bill on the counter and threw open the door as he watched steam lifting from the snow, and more importantly, the side of his truck, in the pale light.

"What the fuck!" the heavy set trucker bellowed as he power marched toward Mark. Jack stood nearby, watching the scene from beyond Mark's shoulder.

"Golden Car Wash today sir?" Mark laughed, finishing his prank with a quick zipping up of his pants and a buttoning of the fly. He turned to face the approaching anger of this bastion of the American highway, a man consumed with rage.

Mark clenched his fists as the trucker lunged toward him. Jack sprang into action, trying to get between the two. Mark and the trucker sandwiched Jack between them as they collided in the snowstorm. The combined inertia of the three bodies clashing together as one overcame the traction in the two inches of snow on the ground, and the group toppled toward the ground.

Jack hit the ground first, face down on the snow covered pavement. Two inches of fresh snow will never be enough to keep someone from hitting the surface of the concrete beneath the white powder. As Jack finished his initial contact with the ground, both Mark and the trucker landed on top of him, driving his face into the ground again. They started laying punches into each other as they rolled to the right. Jack stayed where he had landed, face down in the first snow of the season.

Bouncers poured out of the Wayfarer and separated the two men before attending to Jack. The 9-1-1 call rang out within thirty seconds of the conclusion of the scuffle, but the bouncers couldn't do anything but roll Jack over onto his back and wait. Nobody who works for a watering hole has the training to save someone from a broken neck. I've never met a beer jockey yet who could have saved my brother.

I remember getting the call from Dad at about three in the morning. Dad's voice sounded hoarse from trying to choke back the anguish in his heart. Jack may not have been his true son, he may not have been the best person ever, but Jack always was family and always will be sorely missed. I only experienced life with one brother, and Jack earned my love for him. I know there's nothing different from my end that would have saved Jack, but someday I may forgive myself for that.

CHAPTER 32

Erin's story after that adventure on Baffert Island carried more twists and turns than the largest thrill ride at any amusement park. She left for New York within a couple weeks of our trip, leaving without saying farewell to any of us. The stress of our experience and the aftermath in her relationships with each of us overwhelmed her to the point of driving her away. She left to attend school at Syracuse, the one place she always told us she refused to attend based on the atmosphere and distance from family. Once there, she soon settled in with the party crowd, constantly drenching herself in a cycle of mixers, booze, and frat boys intent on sexual conquest.

Erin was no idiot and kept her guard up at all times. I heard from her on occasion, mostly through e-mail, and every time she recounted tales of delusional men attempting to defrock her and the comical results of their feeble efforts. She often mentioned how she missed the good old days, but as the e-mails continued to come, they grew shorter and less interesting. Also, they began to tell a tale of a hopelessly lonely person. Erin skipped from man to man, falling for false hope in the form of a glowing smile and a kind word. Messages and talks came less and less frequently as the list of broken relationships grew.

Finally, after about a year and a half at school, the messages ceased altogether. I wrote a few times, but never got responses back. I called her folks, but they told me Erin's behavior toward me extended to them as well. She had dedicated herself to a new man and, according to her parents, no longer required memories of the past to make her happy. This new man brought her joy and she planned to marry.

I forgot about Erin for awhile, letting my grief over the loss of her friendship fade behind my studies and two relationships of my own. The first, to Nicole Ames, lasted eight months before I woke up and realized I wanted more from a woman than big breasts, a constantly available partner, and a whiny voice that could peel paint. Sure we had our fun, but her problem came from the fact that she questioned everything. She always worried about the most minute detail and blew the tiniest misstep by me into a gargantuan fight. She'd call and bitch me out for an hour or more one night, then show up the next day and act like nothing happened. I managed to cut that relationship short and move on without much pain in my heart. I never regretted dating her, but I regret cutting her loose even less.

The second girl, Gwen Thomas, I truly loved. Her chestnut hair almost matched the color of my own locks, and she lived and died for the Celtics, Bruins, and Red Sox. Our personalities intertwined almost to the point of freakish proportions, with us sharing similar views on everything from the movies we liked to who we voted for in elections. Gwen and I studied different things, but even those things somehow linked to one another. She focused on World Cultures while I studied Literature, narrowing my expertise to the folklore of nomadic cultures in Europe and North America. We proved inseparable until that day when Gwen moved away.

Since Gwen was three years older than me, she graduated before I even saw the prospect of my degree on the horizon. She quickly gained employment at a high school near Burlington, Vermont, and while a train ride between there and Maine doesn't sound like a terrible struggle, the fact is that doing that proved difficult. Gwen found it hard to fathom because she lacked the pressing need to answer to professors and deadlines.

Don't get me wrong, I know that love is supposed to conquer all, and I'll get back to that notion in a little bit. Despite my best efforts and repeated attempts to make those trips, the distance became too tough to overcome. It seemed that each time I took the train down to her for the weekend, I was met with a series of arguments stemming from her preconceived beliefs that I didn't take the relationship seriously, that I didn't love her because if I did I would move closer to her or find a way to be with her every day. Each time I rode that train back home I found myself a little sadder, a bit angrier, and a tad more confused. What was I doing wrong? I loved her, shouldn't that be enough? Anyway, after a few months of damaging myself with these trips, I decided to end the madness. It helped that Gwen felt the same way.

We still find time to talk to each other occasionally. This e-mail thing is the godsend of the last fifteen years. Gwen is now Gwen Sanders, marrying a nice gentleman named Brent from Seattle a couple years ago. I really enjoyed that ceremony and was happy that Gwen found her a great guy. The Sanders live in Minneapolis now, her teaching and him working in a public relations firm. Their first son is due in a couple months.

My life changed again forever one rainy April night during my fifth year of college, April sixth. I worked on a term paper at my desk when the doorbell rang. I thought nothing of it since my doorbell rang, on average, about six times an evening. People always stopped by either to see Mark Bentley or to ask for tutoring help from me. I carried a reputation around campus as the person to chew the fat with if stuck on a problem with course work. Sometimes this person is called a nerd, but in my case I was respected for my general knowledge, or was it because I played the game better than most? Whatever the case, I dealt with the caller as I did with any other.

"Door's open!" I yelled, knowing that whoever stood on the stoop could hear me through the thin walls of the apartment.

The door didn't open.

"Come in!" I called.

The door still remained shut. A hollow knock echoed off the door.

I rose from my chair and walked slowly to the door. I turned the knob, pulled back on it, and opened the threshold. The person outside dropped my jaw and erupted my eyes from my head in absolute shock.

Erin.

"H-hey," I stammered, not knowing what to think. Erin dripped rain from her coat, a yellow slicker three-quarter length jacket. Her hair was matted to her head, weighed down from the torrent outside. Strawberry blonde locks clung to each cheek and her forehead. Both hands were thrust into her jeans pockets, and she stood with her weight shifted on her left leg.

"Hi," she replied. Her breath lofted into the glow of the exterior lamp. Silence followed that breath as we each looked at the other.

"Hi," I said, breaking the uneasy quiet. A million thoughts flashed through my head. What did she want? Was this right? Was I back home? Was this a joke? What's going on?

"How are you?" she asked. So far, our conversation had stayed monotone. Every word sounded exactly like the others. I wanted to ask all my questions at once, to say everything that I had held in for four years.

"How are you?" I replied.

We both blinked, she shifted her weight. Our eyes locked again, the first time in nearly five years. After a breath, we both laughed.

"Come in," I giggled, "I'll get you a towel."

"Thanks, Jared." She dropped her wet jacket from her shoulders, leaving it in a dripping heap in the doorway. She wore this charcoal gray knit shawl underneath that I remember always thinking only absolutely beautiful girls wore. I gave her one of three clean towels in the apartment, one of Mark's. She dried her hair while sitting on the futon, and she and I talked until dawn, even after Mark came home and went to bed and arose again.

Erin told me she needed a return to the happiness she had from her youth. Her relationship crumbled, she said, when her boyfriend never asked for her hand. He continued to pretend their relationship remained in the early stages, where love meant everything and all other things came second. He also exhibited signs of jealousy, condemning her whenever she talked to another man or did something without him. She said he stopped short of calling her a slut or anything like that, but his constant overbearing attitude on her created a rift that she at first tried to repair but then gave up and accepted. It took her a long time to leave, she told me, because she wanted so badly to possess her dream of a husband and father for her children.

I stayed up with her, through the tears, the questions, the revelations of her life. I knew no other way to deal with her. The problems she carried were definitely beyond my realm of understanding, but as her friend I couldn't help but give her all my support. After that night, I knew Erin's life had to change for the better.

I believe in many old sayings, mainly because they wouldn't be old sayings if not steeped in truth over generations. Perhaps my favorite old saying is love conquers all. I firmly hold on to the notion that loving somebody will undoubtedly triumph over any of life's problems that may arise. Only true, pure love, the kind that binds parents to children, children to pets, friends to friends, and lovers to lovers, can overcome all obstacles. Gwen and I failed because we never truly shared this bond. We came very close, but for whatever reason we missed some small piece that kept us from completing the link. For whatever reason, we failed to complete the puzzle, to put together the future we both wanted to share, a future as one party.

Not so with me and Erin.

We'd always been friends, and ever since that night on the beach at the Dome of the Rock, I'd never forgotten about her. She may have slipped toward the back of my mind, but she never left my thoughts. I can't count how many nights I rehashed my memories of her and deprived myself of sleep. We'd grown from torturing bugs and stealing blueberries through our toughest years and into the rest of our lives together. That concept of sharing the remainder of our lives together caused me to kiss her for the first time all over again, the next day when I took her to visit Dad at the old house in Brandh.

When she kissed me back, I knew my life now meant something. Then, when she told me one sentence a late July evening, I knew my life now meant everything.

She said, "I came back to you because I am ready to say 'Why not.'"

Ten months after giving Erin the only gift she truly wanted, my name, she gave me my first son. We both agreed to name him for something near and dear to both of us, something that meant the world to us because of its importance in both our lives. We named our son Brandhon because it sounded good, but more importantly, because the blessing of our son will always remind us of where we came from and why we love each other more than life itself. Thanks to our years in Brandh, Erin and I will forever share life. Together.

CHAPTER 33

Compared to the rest of us, my father led an unassuming life after our adventure, returning to work at the university that fall and resuming his work in the education field. He attempted to find Ragnarok on two more expeditions to islands neighboring Dome of the Rock, but his efforts remained unfulfilled. Dad retreated into a deeper shell with each failure. At the same time, his health continued to fade. His glaucoma tore the sight from his right eye, leaving him legally blind in it about three years ago. Glaucoma also began to attack Dad's left eye and slowly stole the sight from that eye as well. Jack and I employed a caretaker for Dad, with me taking over responsibility for that upon Jack's untimely demise.

In fact, I think that Jack's death caused Dad to go downhill. He never escaped the grasp of the grief from that event, not fully. Dad constantly blamed himself for forcing Jack into the life Jack chose, believing he was responsible for the decisions Jack made as a misbegotten teen. Dad also dreaded never getting the chance to tell Jack how proud he was to call Jack his son. I often told Dad that Jack knew he loved him, but Dad, as was his way, didn't listen.

Eight days ago, I received a call from the hospital in Bangor. Dad suffered from a massive heart attack and barely clung to life. I raced to the scene immediately, by myself. When I got there Dad remarkably held consciousness.

"Pickle," he spoke, barely audibly. He pushed his words through a respirator attached to him.

"Dad," I choked through my welling tears.

"Pickle, I love you."

"I love you, Dad." The tears in my eyes broke and poured down my cheeks.

"Never forget where you come from son." Dad coughed after these words.

His coughing forced me to look at him. Until that point, I lacked the courage to look upon my dying father. I stared into the floor until his coughing caught my attention. I looked up from the floor and into his eyes, witnessing sadness where an overwhelming joy of life once lived. He looked back at me, and for a moment I forgot how he probably couldn't see me, even with his glasses on.

"Pickle, without you I was nothing. Thank you."

"No, Dad. You were never nothing."

"Thanks, son." Dad rose at the waist, lifting himself almost to a seated position. He pushed his right hand to his brow, extended it toward me, and pressed it against his brow again. After completing his salute, he slumped back into the bed exhausted. A tear rolled down his left cheek.

"Thank you, Dad." My eyes burned with sticky tears.

Dad coughed again then said the words I will never shake from my memory.

"Pickle, don't forget this. I will see you again."

He collapsed into the pillow after this sentence and closed his eyes. His lungs expanded one time, and with the exhalation Dad left me to go join Mom once more. I kissed him softly on the forehead before Dr. Spencer answered the emergency call. As Dr. Spencer made every attempt to revive my father, I backed out of the room and let the tears stream from my eyes.

My father, Dr. Seamus McCracken, passed away the same way he lived, with nobility, with grace, and without anger. I will miss him forever.

CHAPTER 34

After Dad's death, I quickly threw together arrangements for Dad's cremation, as he requested months before in his living will. He wanted no burial plot and no memorial. Instead, Dad wished to have his ashes spread where he felt that the greatest disappointment of his life and the turning point of his offspring's lives occurred. He longed to sleep eternally at Baffert Island, at the Dome of the Rock.

I can't fully explain his reasoning behind the choice of after death ritual. After all, we never found anything resembling the gates to Asgard at Baffert Island. The whole expedition there proved fruitless. Still, as far as I can tell, Dad still believed that something about that place held the secret to his lifelong quest. Perhaps, I can only surmise, Dad thought that he could still fulfill his dream, even in death. Maybe he wished that the valkyries would come to claim him if they could only find him. Whatever the reason, Dad wanted it that way.

Brandhon and I set out for Dome of the Rock on Saturday morning. Brandhon, bless his heart, never lacks enthusiasm for adventure. He'll make a great explorer someday, just like his grandfather. A nearly constant repetitive "When will we be there?" exited his lips as we drove from home through the countryside and toward the ferry dock.

I admit that I lacked his excitement. After all, the reason for going back to Baffert wasn't exactly a pleasure cruise. The two of us rode that two-lane highway with one purpose in mind, and that was to say good-bye to Grampy. Okay, counting Dad we carried three in the car.

I don't remember much about the ferry ride over. The ferry service only came into being a couple years back as a result of a reclamation project by Governor Levitan. The boulders were cleared from the southern portion of the channel between the mainland and the island, making it safe for floating transportation to pass through to the park. Dad and I both joined the governor in lobbying for this action, as we felt that the idea carried great merit from an educational standpoint.

Dome of the Rock State Park welcomes people from across the region every year, especially in the summer months when vacationing families like to frequent the site. There aren't many active volcanic sites along the Eastern seaboard, and the novelty of a natural disaster in one's backyard seems to attract all walks of life. Plus, the sand beach along the western shore provides the backdrop for one of the most popular public beaches in central Maine, as well as one of the nicest views around, especially at dusk as the sun slips over the horizon.

Nothing much had changed since my last visit. The same trail still cut through the crater floor, running its path across the underbrush. After the mile and a half hike, you still crested a hill that overlooks the lush valley floor. A dense canopy of brush still stretched across the lava dome, clear to the eastern wall. The floor of the crater did appear to have sunken a little, no doubt the aftereffects of the eruption I survived. Serpent Rock watched over the floor from its perch on the top of the eastern face, just like in the last visit, still guarding the entrance to the cave beneath it on the hillside. That is, if the lava we escaped hadn't filled that cave, which is now actually a large scar across the facade of the bluff.

Brandhon and I arrived at the visitor's center early in the afternoon. We followed the trail to the area where Tanner had checked one of his instruments, the spot where the gully wash cut across the trail.

"What do you think of that, Brandhon?" I asked, pointing to the expansive valley to the left of the trail.

I heard no answer.

"What do you think, Brandhon?"

I turned to look behind me. Brandhon wasn't there.

"Brandhon? Where are you?" I called over the breeze coming down through the crater. I started to grow clammy and felt a lump of terror rising in my throat.

"Brandhon?"

I turned to my left, toward the valley, when I heard branches snapping. The snapping came closer to the trail from within the underbrush. The wind stopped blowing completely as a four-year-old's head popped out of the bushes with a look of glee on his face.

"Daddy!" Brandhon grinned.

"Brandhon, come here," I replied.

Brandhon stayed in the bushes.

"Now."

"I want to play on the toys."

"Toys?" I scratched my chin.

"I found play toys."

Brandhon ducked into a spot in the brush. I called for him to come back, but he ignored me and gave me no choice. I entered the thicket where Brandhon disappeared.

Upon cracking the interior, I discovered a path to crawl through. I followed the winding course on my hands and knees, quickly scrambling within the deep wall of plant life. I kept my eyes forward, trying to catch sight of Brandhon in front of me. Crawling proved more difficult as I started heading down a slope, so I flipped to my rear and slid down the hillside on my feet. The ground leveled out and I soon found room to stand.

I rose to my feet and found myself at the mouth of a canyon. Both sides of this canyon extended nearly perpendicular to the ground. I could see gnarled branches and bushes stretching across the top of the canyon, more than twenty feet above my head. Brandhon waited for me at the entrance to this undiscovered pocket within the earth, bouncing with excitement.

"See, Dad. Play toys! Play toys!"

Brandhon tugged at my sleeve with his left hand and pointed toward the far end of the canyon with his right. I brushed dust from my knees and lifted my gaze to where Brandhon was pointing. I gulped when I saw what lay before me.

"Stay here, Brandhon."

I stepped forward cautiously, slowly taking one step and waiting before taking the next. The sight before me awed me to no end. Mainly, I wanted to make sure I wasn't hallucinating.

"This is it," I muttered to myself. "I found it."

The structure in front of me stood at the enclosed end of the canyon. Its gilded face shimmered intensely where sunlight peeked through the brush canopy and impacted it. The entire site appeared to be covered in precious metals and gems. A marble slab about twenty-five feet long and twelve feet deep created the foundation. Twin columns of what looked to be solid gold rose on either side. A second step, also of gold, lay between these pillars, resting atop the marble slab. An ornate lattice twisted between the two columns across the top. In the center of this lattice, a rooster, carved entirely of translucent reddish rock, ruby perhaps, sat perched over what was unquestionably a gate of some kind. I swallowed hard.

"The gate," I whispered.

Then something happened that I still find hard to believe. Outside the two columns, on either side, I spotted two large statues. Carved from a green stone, either jade or emerald, two wolves guarded the gate with a menacing look upon their collective visages. They stood on their haunches, obviously fashioned that way to frighten members of a past culture. Each looked ready to devour anyone foolish enough to tread on the hallowed land they protected.

Then I watched them move.

They slowly closed their mouths first, so I thought my mind was playing a trick on me. But then they hopped down from where they stood and crossed paths before taking the other's spot on the altar. Brandhon ducked behind me and wrapped his arms around my left leg.

"It's okay," I assured him. "They can't hurt us." Hey, if I said it out loud, maybe it would be true.

The two wolves gained position and stopped moving, save for the slow flipping of their respective tails. Brandhon let go of my leg as I removed my backpack. I unzipped it and removed Dad's urn from within its main pouch.

"Dad, I'll never forget everything you were to me. I think you're going to like it here."

I lifted the lid from the urn and slowly poured the ashes from it. As I started, a breeze picked up around me. The breeze became a dust devil, catching the ashes in its wind before one particle touched the ground. I quickly flashed a glance to the brush behind me.

It remained dead still. No breeze blew through any other part of the clearing or the canyon.

The swirling wind kicked Dad's ashes around within it, moving them faster and faster and closer together. The dust devil then advanced toward the gate, carrying every particle with it. As it reached the gate itself, I noticed that the contents of the urn began to resemble a shape, something I thought I'd never see again.

"Dad," I choked from my swelling throat. Tears welled in my eyes.

The swirling wind stopped at the entrance to the gate, holding in place as the shape in the cloud of particles continued to stay intact. Then, the shape within the wind moved itself.

It seemed to raise part of itself toward what appeared to be the head. It pressed the particle limb to its brow, extended it toward me, and pressed it back. As it did this, I heard a whisper echo across the canyon wall.
"I love you, Pickle."
Then, just as suddenly as it came up, the whirlwind vanished. The ashes disappeared with the dust devil. They simply disappeared. Brandhon hugged me around my waist as I stood there quiet for a few moments.
"Say good-bye, Brandhon."
"Good-bye, Grampy."
We backtracked from the clearing and returned up the trail we entered from. My eyes swelled red with uncried tears as I climbed from the crater's floor. As we reached the trail once more, I looked up to the eastern wall, to Serpent Rock. The snake shaped boulder returned the gaze, staring down like it had for generations.
I blinked once then mouthed three words to it.
"I beat you."
With that, I clutched Brandhon's hand in mine, and the two of us hiked back to the visitor's center and took the next ferry ride back to land.
You're the first person I've told about all this. I know living it is something I will never forget. Then again, why would I choose to?
Dad was right when he told me that every person has a story and each of us should live that story out. I followed his advice, lived my story, and that has made all the difference.

Also available from PublishAmerica
TEENAGER RULES OR TEENAGERS RULE
by Tee Stuppiello

Teenager Rules or Teenagers Rule is a lighthearted, fun and real look at issues teens are dealing with today. It is filled with stories and "rules" acting as advice to help make it easier for pre-teens and teenagers to get through some of the most difficult times a girl may have to go through. Coming from the viewpoint of other teenagers, girls can easily relate to the stories and lessons that are meant to encourage self-esteem and make them aware of their own unique beauty, strength and the understanding they are not alone. With eight chapters in total, each created as a "handbook," they contain insightful, fun tales and "rules" to follow on being popular, being beautiful, getting away with lies, making a boy jealous, making a best friend, dealing with bullies and other teenage situations.

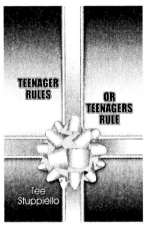

Paperback, 61 pages
6" x 9"
ISBN 1-60672-805-9

About the author:

Tee Stuppiello spent her childhood in central New Jersey where she resides with her daughters, Melody and Toni Lee, and fiancé, Bryan. The idea for *Teenager Rules or Teenagers Rule* came to her while spending time with her teenage daughter and her friends on a snowy winter day. She is in the process of writing *Teenagers Volume 2* and other stories.

Available to all bookstores nationwide.
www.publishamerica.com

Also available from PublishAmerica

THE HAND THAT SCARED JENNY

by Beverly Rosas

Whose hand did Jenny see reaching over the top of the backyard fence? Was it the wicked witch down the street? Was it the mysterious kidnapper? Jenny began an investigation, uncovering a shocking surprise.

Paperback, 46 pages
8.5" x 8.5"
ISBN 1-4241-9138-6

About the author:

Beverly Rosas is a special education teacher who works with children that have learning disabilities. Throughout her childhood, she approached every day as a new adventure. She sees that same sense of imagination in many of her students, and wants to encourage it in every child. This book is her way of inspiring that spark of imagination that is in us all.

Available to all bookstores nationwide.
www.publishamerica.com

Also available from PublishAmerica

SERENITY ISLE
by Adriana Vasquez

Serenity Isle is for the angry soul, the bitter heart that wonders for the answers in life. Healing is the question, the deepest sentiment within our heart waiting to explode from within. Emotions throughout life with love, with parents, with life as a whole that leaves scars in our heart. These poems comment meaningfully on life's sorrows, depressions and its hard moments...

The purpose is to help the reader see things the way life is, and despite all the problems we have in life it reassures the reader there is a light at the end of the tunnel.

Paperback, 132 pages
5.5" x 8.5"
ISBN 1-60610-509-4

About the author:

Adriana Vasquez Becerril was born in New York City. She currently works as a school principal in the Bronx, with a Ph.D. in school leadership from St. Johns University. Adriana has written other books like *Passages of Life*.

Available to all bookstores nationwide.
www.publishamerica.com

Also available from PublishAmerica

BARS, BEAM, FLOOR, VAULT, DEATH
by Diana Danali

Bars, Beam, Floor, Vault, Death is the story of a mother's need to bring to justice the gymnastics coach who abused her young daughters. Morgan Jensen, Kate Anderson, and Julie Murphy tolerate Tom Connor's cruelty for some time before realizing that he is practicing mind control on their innocent daughters. After finally rescuing their daughters from him, while risking their lives, they embark on a mission to discover who he really is and stop his evil ways. While on their journey of discovery they learn that he has changed his name and is a suspect in the murder of an eleven-year-old girl who trained at his former gymnastics facility. The three women encounter people from his past and gain the information they need to put an end to his abuse. They return to Colorado thinking they have enough evidence to confront the coach. However, Tom Connor proves to be more cunning than they had ever imagined.

Paperback, 160 pages
5.5" x 8.5"
ISBN 1-60610-467-5

About the author:

Diana Danali was born and raised in Canon City, Colorado, and has lived there most of her life. She was a gymnastics instructor for two years. For the past twelve years she has been a Curves multi-club owner and for two of those years she was also a mentor for Curves International, Inc. She opened the thirteenth Curves club in the world in Canon City in 1996. With the help of Curves International, Inc., she was instrumental in installing Curves circuits in the five women's correctional facilities in Colorado. She is currently working on her second manuscript.

Available to all bookstores nationwide.
www.publishamerica.com